MURDER ON THE SS ROSA

A GINGER GOLD MYSTERY

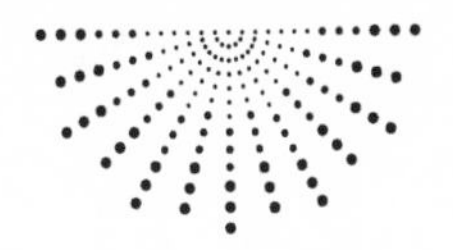

LEE STRAUSS

MURDER ON THE SS ROSA

A GINGER GOLD MYSTERY

COPYRIGHT

THIS BOOK USES BRITISH SPELLING

Murder on the SS Rosa

Cover by Steven Novak

Illustrations by Tasia Strauss

La Plume Press

3205-415 Commonwealth Road

Kelowna, BC, Canada

V4V 2M4

www.laplumepress.com

ISBN: 978-1988677606

Printed in the United States

PRAISE FOR GINGER GOLD

"Clever and entertaining, you'll love this charming Golden Age mystery series. And the fashion is to die for!" **- Molly C. Quinn, actress, *Castle***

"I rank Lee Strauss as the best living cozy mystery writer. Her characters are believable but interesting, her stories are fun to follow and her use of language is superb. She makes the 1920s come alive in my imagination. **I constantly read cozies and Lee's Lady Gold Mysteries are the very best."** - LoriLynn, Amazon reviewer

"Another deftly crafted mystery by the master of the genre..." Midwest Book Review

GINGER GOLD MYSTERIES

(IN ORDER)

Murder on the SS *Rosa*
Murder at Hartigan House
Murder at Bray Manor
Murder at Feathers & Flair
Murder at the Mortuary
Murder at Kensington Gardens
Murder at St. George's Church
The Wedding of Ginger & Basil
Murder Aboard the Flying Scotsman
Murder at the Boat Club
Murder on Eaton Square
Murder by Plum Pudding
Murder on Fleet Street
Murder at Brighton Beach
Murder in Hyde Park
Murder at the Royal Albert Hall
Murder in Belgravia
Murder on Mallowan Court
Murder at the Savoy

Murder at the Circus
Murder at the Boxing Club
Murder in France

CHAPTER ONE

In the dismal autumn of the last year of the Great War, Ginger Gold had vowed she'd never go back to Europe. Yet here she was, five years later in 1923, aboard the SS *Rosa* as it traversed the Atlantic from Boston to Liverpool.

"Isn't a dinner invitation from the captain reserved for *very important persons*?" Haley Higgins asked.

Ginger propped a hand on her tiny waist and feigned insult. "Are you suggesting that I'm not a very important person?"

"I'd never suggest such a thing," Haley said lightly. "Only that I'm not aware of your connection to him."

"Oh, yes. Father used to travel to England once or twice a year for business, and they had made an acquaintance. Of course, this was some years ago, before Father fell ill. Captain Walsh recognised my name on the passenger list. It was nice of him to extend an invitation, was it not?"

Haley nodded. "I expect it to be quite entertaining."

Ginger chose a billowy, violet dropped-waist frock with a hem that ended near her ankles, nude stockings with seams that ran up the back of her slender legs, and black designer T-strap heels. She clipped on dangling earrings and patted the ends of her bobbed red hair with the palms of her gloved hands. She made a show of presenting herself.

"How do I look?"

"Gorgeous, as always," Haley said. Long since dressed, she waited patiently in a rose-coloured upholstered chair. She was the sensible type, having only packed a few tweed and linen suits. She wasn't much for "presentation." It made getting ready quick and painless.

Curled up on the silky pink quilted cover on Ginger's bed was a small, short-haired black and white dog. Ginger scrubbed him behind his pointed ears and kissed his forehead. "You're such a good boy, Boss." The Boston terrier's stub of a tail wagged in agreement.

Ginger finished her ensemble by draping a creamy silk shawl over her shoulders. "Shall we?" Ginger said, motioning to the door.

Boss stood and stretched his hind legs.

"Oh, sorry, Bossy. Not you this time."

The dog let out a snort of disappointment, then circled his pillow before settling and swiftly fell back to sleep.

"I love the sea! Don't you?" Ginger said as she and Haley walked along an exterior corridor of the ship. She extended her youthful arms and inhaled exuberantly. "It's one of the reasons I love Boston. So invigorating. Makes one feel alive!"

"Oh, honey, listen to you!" Haley said with amusement. "Your latent Britishness is becoming more pronounced the closer we get to England. Mimicking Ginger's sudden use of an English accent, she added, "Makes *one* feel alive."

Though Ginger considered herself a Bostonian through

and through, she embraced her English heritage. After all, Massachusetts *was* part of New *England*.

"You're jolly well right, old thing," Ginger admitted with an exaggerated English accent. She laughed heartily, bringing a smile to Haley's normally stoic expression.

"You sounded like your father just now," Haley said.

Ginger placed a hand on her heart. "Oh, I do miss him."

"Me, too."

"In his honour I shall be thoroughly British for the duration of my time abroad."

A smile spread across Haley's wide face. "And you'll do it charmingly."

Ginger threaded her arm through her friend's. "Soon-to-be Doctor Higgins," she said. "We mustn't keep the captain waiting."

"If you insist, Mrs. Gold," Haley returned, then added, "You know, I think the captain has eyes for you."

"*Pffft*. How can you say that? We only met him for a second." Ginger flicked her gloved hand. "Besides, he's got a wife."

"With men like the captain," Haley said stiffly, "I hardly think that matters."

* * *

A wide, modern staircase with lush red carpeting led to an elegant first-class dining room on the top deck.

"Posh," Haley said. "I'm not sure I fit in here."

"Nonsense," Ginger responded airily. "You're with me!"

Haley scoffed lightly. "An accessory? I'm certainly not flamboyant enough to suit your style."

Ginger laughed, a spritely laugh her husband, Daniel,

once had said reminded him of fairies dancing in a waterfall.

"You are on the inside, my dear Haley. That's what counts."

The red carpet continued throughout the restaurant, accenting jade-green and dusty rose upholstered chairs placed in groups of four around round, brass-trimmed chestnut tables.

"There they are," Ginger said, and led the way to where their hosts were seated.

Captain Walsh was an attractive man of average height and weight. His thick dark hair was greying slightly at the temples. He stood when he identified them, exuding authority. "Mrs. Gold. It's a pleasure."

"The pleasure is ours," Ginger said, shaking the captain's hand. His palm was large but soft, and he wore a wide ring that brandished a flat section of jade. The sleeve of his shirt slipped past the four stripes on the cuff of his jacket, and Ginger noted a handsome cuff link, a shiny silver piece embossed with a fleur-de-lis.

Motioning to Haley, she added, "This is my companion, Miss Higgins."

The captain's smile remained as he offered his hand. "Good to meet you."

Haley shook his hand with vice-grip confidence. "Likewise."

"May I introduce my wife, Mrs. Walsh." The thin woman on his right wore a dated late-Edwardian smock that was cinched at the waist. Her overly upright posture indicated that she most certainly wore an antiquated corset. She nodded in greeting, but refrained from offering a hand or even a smile. Ginger blamed the corset for her poor temperament.

"Nice to meet you, Mrs. Walsh." Ginger took the seat next to the captain while Haley positioned herself beside his wife.

"Please let me express my appreciation at your kind invitation to join you on our first night," Ginger said. "I'm sure these seats are much coveted!"

"It is my delight to have the daughter of Mr. Hartigan onboard. Your father was a respectable gentleman, and I'm honoured to have known him. I only wish he were alive and with us here today."

"As do I." Ginger patted Haley's arm. "Miss Higgins, his personal nurse through his last years, showed him the compassion and respect he deserved. She was also a tremendous comfort to my little sister and stepmother. I really don't know what we would've done without her." Ginger's praise of Haley was sincere, but she also hoped a good character reference would erase any prejudice forthcoming due to her friend's unorthodox attire.

"How fortunate that she could accompany you to London," Mrs. Walsh said with a crisp English accent.

"Indeed, it is stupendously good fortune," Ginger said. "Just as I was making plans to attend to my father's London estate, Miss Higgins learned she would continue her medical training there."

Mrs. Walsh looked astounded. "A lady doctor?"

"Many doors are opening for the modern woman, Mrs. Walsh," Haley responded. "In fact, the institution in question is the London School of Medicine for Women."

"But why London?" Captain Walsh asked. "Though I'm the first to acknowledge how fine the city is, surely there is a prestigious facility in America?"

"Yes, of course," Haley said. "I completed two years at Boston University before enlisting in the war." A shadow flickered behind her eyes. "You could say I was ready for a change of scenery." The catalyst for change was Haley's fiancé, who, despite potential social repercussions, had unceremoniously broken off their relationship to pursue another woman.

Before the captain or Mrs. Walsh could probe further, Ginger interjected, "Miss Higgins served as a nurse during the war, both in France and England. She developed an affection for London, didn't you, *old girl*?"

Ginger laughed at her use of the English parlance, and Haley smirked. "I did, indeed."

A waiter took their drink orders, and when he returned, Ginger accepted her glass of fine French wine with relish. "Even though we're no longer in the States, I can't help but feel guilty." She cast a slight glance over her shoulder and laughed. "I half-expect a federal Prohibition agent to arrest me any minute!"

"You are quite safe," Captain Walsh said with a smile. "This vessel is under the command of His Royal Highness, who, on occasion, happens to enjoy a drink or two."

Ginger sipped daintily as she allowed the fruity sensation to tingle her mouth before swallowing. She sighed with contentment.

Mrs. Walsh attempted to pick up her glass, but the captain moved it out of reach. "Not for you. You know what occurs when you drink too much." Mrs. Walsh's lips pursed in anger, but she stayed silent.

Ginger and Haley shared a look. If the captain was watching out for his wife, he certainly wasn't subtle. The heat of Mrs. Walsh's embarrassment stretched across the table.

Thankfully, the meal arrived, dissipating the situation. Ginger's mouth watered at the sight of roasted lamb with mint sauce, roast potatoes, and buttered green beans. The smell was heavenly. The chief cook, a rotund man with a ruddy complexion and dark eyes, hovered beside the captain, waiting for his assessment.

Captain Walsh made a point of chewing well, and followed the morsel up with a sip of chardonnay. "It's good, Babineaux."

After her first bite, Ginger added enthusiastically, "Simply delicious!"

Babineaux ducked his chin, then cast a glance at Mrs. Walsh. A look passed between them as the woman nodded her approval, allowing for a smile. Had Ginger imagined it, or had something more meaningful than a culinary rating been communicated?

A beautiful woman sat at a table across the room. Ginger recognised her as Nancy Guilford, the famous American actress. In her company were several gentlemen —one Ginger thought to be particularly dapper—and a middle-aged female companion. Ginger admired Miss Guilford's exotic, long-waisted ocean-blue oriental gown trimmed in fur. Her wavy blonde bob exposed diamond earrings that glistened in the electric light, and her lips were thick and bright red.

"Patty, darlin'," Nancy Guilford said with a loud New Jersey accent. Her voice was surprisingly nasal. Not at all what a person would expect from such a beautiful and sophisticated face. "Hand me my ciggies."

Her companion delivered a package of cigarettes, which Miss Guilford opened with graceful fingers. She placed a cigarette into an ivory-coloured holder and held it to her lips. One of the men (not the dapper one, Ginger was happy to note) rapidly produced a brass lighter and offered a flame.

Miss Guilford inhaled, then let out a long stream of smoke in the captain's direction.

Though it was a simple, routine, everyday activity—a mere inhale and exhale—Nancy Guilford had made a compelling performance out of it. Even if someone present hadn't recognised the actress, her flair and charisma commanded attention. Ginger was sure the entire room had noticed her. Mrs. Walsh in particular seemed agitated. She glared at Miss Guilford with jealousy and suspicion in her eyes.

Ginger didn't think Mrs. Walsh was being paranoid in the least. The blonde stared shamelessly at the captain, going out of her way to present a creamy, *bare* calf when she crossed her legs.

Oh, mercy.

Captain Walsh pulled at his collar and pretended not to notice. The four of them returned to polite conversation, interspersed with comments on the quality of the food and the splendour of the dining room.

Throughout the meal, the captain, when his eyes weren't straying to the glamorous actress, watched Ginger in a way that left her feeling slightly uncomfortable. She feared Haley's assessment of him was all too correct.

CHAPTER TWO

"That was an interesting evening, wasn't it?" Ginger said when she and Haley returned to their stateroom.

Haley agreed. "It was."

Ginger began the process of undressing, motioning to Haley to assist her by unzipping her dress. "The actress had eyes for the captain, and the chef—did you see the way he watched the captain's wife?"

"A convoluted affair."

"Great entertainment, though, wouldn't you say?"

Haley nodded. "I would."

Ginger couldn't rest until she'd finished unpacking. Disgruntled, she stared at her three large trunks, four suit-cases, and a dozen hat boxes. Of course, it wasn't necessary for her to unpack everything for a five-day journey, but if she didn't, the odious smell of pine and mothballs would most certainly be ingrained in the fibres of her wardrobe before she reached London, and that just wouldn't do.

"Molly usually cares for this," Ginger said. "Her fear of

deep water was too great a barrier, and she refused to accompany me. I guess I can't blame her for that."

"I could assist," Haley said, "though I'm not much attuned to fashion."

"Your help would be so appreciated!" Ginger said. "The only skill required is the ability to arrange garments on a hanger. Day dresses together, starting on the left in the wardrobe, followed by tea dresses and evening wear."

"I'm afraid I don't know the difference."

"Really, Haley?" Ginger wasn't sure if her friend was serious or in jest. "Very well. This is a day dress." Ginger held up a simple streamline cotton frock in a bright gingham print. She opened up a second trunk and rummaged through the contents to produce an elegant dress with layers of cream chiffon with a wide black sash and taffeta bow. "This is a Jeanne Lanvin, suitable for afternoon tea or semi-formal dining."

"Who's Jeanne Lanvin?"

Ginger stilled. "Only the most innovative, new designer in Paris!"

"Oh, of course," Haley said dryly.

"And this evening gown..." Ginger said with a lilt to her voice, "... is a Coco Chanel, perfect for a night of dancing." She held up a sleeveless, straight-line dress made of rayon that shimmered with layers of sheer crepe silk against her body. The skirt shimmied when Ginger swivelled her hips and had a shocking hemline that ended mid-calf. "Surely you've heard of Coco Chanel?"

Haley shot her an exaggerated look of offence. "I don't live under a rock."

Ginger laughed. She held a deep affection for her travel companion. They'd met in France during the war. Nurse Higgins had single-handedly saved a colleague of Ginger's from certain death—the man had had an unfortunate encounter with a sharp German-made blade. Ginger had introduced herself as Mademoiselle Antoinette LaFleur. Her French citizen persona was so convincing that Haley's jaw nearly hit the floor when they were reacquainted after the Great War in Boston. When it became apparent that her father needed personal care, Ginger specifically sought out Haley. To her credit, Haley accepted Ginger's explanation that Mademoiselle LaFleur was created for the war effort. "She" ended when the war did—and Ginger was unable to speak about it further.

Boss' head bobbed, and he stretched out a small black paw from where he slept at the bottom of Ginger's bed. He yawned in greeting, then promptly closed his eyes and emitted a soft snore.

Ginger changed into her nightwear—a satin jade-green, one-piece teddy trimmed with champagne-coloured lace. Haley donned a plain white camisole and matching bloomers, and unpinned her curly, long brown hair, which twisted up at her neck to create the illusion of a wavy bob. Sitting in front of the dressing table mirror, she brushed out her hair and spoke to Ginger's reflection. "Are you ready, Mrs. Gold?"

"Ready for what?"

"For your new life in London."

"It's been ten years since I've stepped foot there." Ginger's last foray to England had been on her honeymoon in 1913. All of her work during the war took place on the Continent. "I hardly know what to expect."

"The world seems to have changed on a dime," Haley returned. "I imagine we'll both be surprised."

"Surely you must be excited to continue your medical training," Ginger said, secretly envying her friend. Ginger's years studying at Boston University were among her favourite memories. She loved the academic atmosphere and enjoyed the camaraderie of her fellow students. Her studies in languages and math had turned out to be of particular use during the war, but now Ginger felt at a loss at what to do with her time.

"Yes," Haley admitted, "but I think I'll miss Boston."

Ginger twisted a short strand of hair around her index finger to reinforce the curl that turned in towards her cheek. "I'm not sure I'll be away long enough to miss it."

"Oh?" Haley paused mid-brush. "Do tell."

"I might just sell Hartigan House and return to the States. Even though I was born in England, I was only eight years old when Father married Sally and relocated. I'm afraid I'm rather American."

"Indeed, Ginger, you are very American."

"But, as you know, I can be as English as the next Brit when I set my mind to it. Father remained thoroughly English until the day he died."

Haley returned the brush to the dressing table and climbed into her bed. "You are culturally versatile."

"I won't miss Sally one bit," Ginger continued, "though I might become sentimental over Louisa."

"Your half sister is ... memorable."

"She's spoiled, obnoxious, and unbearable is what you mean."

"I would never say it."

"I'll enjoy London, I think, for a while," Ginger said as she burrowed deeper under her covers. "But then what will I do with myself?"

"I'm sure there will be plenty to entertain you."

"To begin with certainly, but then what? At least you

have your career. Boston is my home, but with only Sally to welcome me back, well, it's just not that inviting."

"So, you're divided," Haley said. "Stay in London, where you don't know anyone besides me and risk boredom, or sell Hartigan House and return to Boston, where you have a social circle. But due to that same social circle, you would be obligated to live with your evil step-mother."

"Precisely. Haley Higgins, you are so perceptive."

"It's a skill required of my profession."

"And yet you've managed to not help me at all. I'm no closer to an answer."

"Dear Ginger, you're young, beautiful, and an heiress, ergo there's a good chance you'll meet an eligible bachelor or two. That should keep you entertained. Unless, of course, your feelings for Mr. Wellington go deeper than you let on."

Mr. Wellington was a successful accountant, born and raised in Boston, and a long-suffering suitor. He appeared out of nowhere just days after her official period of mourning over Daniel had ended. A man of virtue and good ethics, any woman would've jumped at a chance to marry him. His look was plain but not homely, his skin quite pale, and his stomach a bit paunchy—likely due to a sedentary lifestyle lived indoors—but not overly so. He valued order and logic and approached life with similar sentiments, having very little appreciation for passion or spontaneity.

The complete opposite of Daniel in every way.

She turned his offer of marriage down in the end, and though she hated to hurt him, she knew they would never make each other happy. Besides, he wanted children, and that was something she just couldn't promise him. Mother Nature had seen to that.

Ginger's mind drifted momentarily to the dapper gentleman she'd witnessed at Miss Guilford's table. Here was a well-dressed man with intelligent eyes that sparked with passion. Ginger played with the gold ring on her finger, which was her habit, then stopped suddenly with a flood of mortification. How could she polish her wedding band whilst pondering the good looks of a stranger!

Boss, sensing his mistress's emotional need, crept to her side as she slipped under the covers, and nuzzled her neck. Ginger whispered, "Oh, Boss, you're such a peach."

She and Haley spent some time reading with the help of the electric lamps beside their beds—Haley with a medical textbook and Ginger with a new Agatha Christie detective novel.

Ginger could have booked separate rooms, but she didn't mind the company, especially with her maid, Molly, staying behind. She gave Haley the option of her own room, but Haley wasn't one to take advantage because Ginger had money. She'd expressed her gratitude on having her passage to London covered in the deal.

Eventually, Ginger's eyes drooped. "I'm ready to call it a day," she said.

Haley flipped the switch next to her bed, and the electric lights extinguished. "Sleep well, Ginger."

"Sleep well, Haley."

Moments later, their peace and quiet was interrupted by a loud zipper sound.

"Boss!" Ginger shouted.

"Dear Lord!" Haley said. "Light a match!"

CHAPTER THREE

The next morning Ginger dropped a copy of *Pearson's* magazine on the table beside her cup of coffee and crumb-laden plate. It was opened to the cross-word page, with every square filled out in ink.

"They're far too easy," Ginger said.

Haley rolled her eyes. "You say that every time."

"It's true every time."

"Then why do you do them?"

"I'm hoping one day, I'll finally be stumped."

Haley paused before saying, "I doubt that'll ever happen. Maybe you should craft them yourself?"

"Now, that's a thought. Still, I'd forfeit the challenge of completing them since I'd already know the answers beforehand."

A waiter returned with a trolley to top up their coffee and to offer another round of fresh croissants and bread. Ginger and Haley had filled up on the English version of breakfast—bacon and eggs—and requested coffee only.

"I suppose we'll have to switch to tea once we're in England," Ginger said.

"I think not," Haley said as she added a healthy dose of cream and two spoons of sugar to her black brew. "My problem will be finding a cup that is strong enough to suit me."

"I love a good cup of coffee, but there is something charming and sophisticated about their fascination with teatime. I quite like holding dainty china cups with my little finger extended." Ginger demonstrated as a lark.

"You'll fit right in, Mrs. Gold."

"Actually, the English frown on the pinky." Ginger laughed, and Haley joined in with a begrudging half grin.

"Are you going to see your in-laws?" Haley asked carefully. She sipped her coffee and kept her eyes averted.

"It's okay to talk about them," Ginger said, noting her friend's discomfort. "And about Daniel."

Haley caught Ginger's eyes but merely nodded.

"It's only Daniel's grandmother, Ambrosia, and his sister, Felicia, who are left, you see. So much tragedy in that family. His parents died in a carriage accident, leaving Daniel and Felicia orphans when Felicia was still an infant. His grandfather died of heart failure before Daniel was even born. When we returned for our honeymoon in '13, Ambrosia was the Lady of Bray Manor and Felicia was only eleven." Ginger frowned. "Daniel was always concerned about his sister not having a proper mother to raise her. He felt terribly guilty about leaving her behind when he came to Boston. I don't think he meant to stay as long as he did. And then the war called him."

"I thought he crossed the Atlantic specifically to meet you?"

"Well, he *was* after the Hartigan money. Before his father died, he'd strapped the family with gambling debts, and Daniel did what he felt he had to in order to save Bray Manor."

"He married you *for money*?" Haley was unable to keep shock from lacing her words.

Ginger eyed her over her cup. "It's not unheard of. My father was in favour. Daniel didn't have money, but he did have a title."

Haley slammed down her half-empty mug. "What? How could you've kept that from me?"

Ginger lifted a shoulder. "As you well know, Americans find British titles pretentious. You do better in business without them. Self-made men are more esteemed than those born into money. Even though Father greatly admired Daniel's title, he never introduced him with it. Besides, Daniel and I ended up falling in love, so it all became a moot point."

"Do *you* have a title?"

Ginger let out a small breath and murmured, "Lady Gold. My husband was a baron. Daniel, Lord Gold."

"Lady Gold!"

"*Shh!* There's no need to draw attention."

"But, Ginger." Haley couldn't keep the chuckle out of her voice. "You're a *Lady*."

Ginger squinted her eyes. "'Mrs. Gold' will do just fine, thank you very much."

The table next to them became occupied by an older couple who seemed to be feeling the effects of the time change already, or perhaps were among the unfortunates whose stomachs failed to cooperate with the ocean crossing. He was wispy thin, as if he ate nothing at all, saving all for his stout and top-heavy wife. Her hair was as white as a sheet, yet styled expertly with marcelled waves. Her maid undoubtedly hadn't refused to accompany *her*. Though the woman's size dictated that her clothing was specially made, Ginger noted the quality of the fabrics and the modern design.

"Mrs. Fairchild," the woman said in a way of introduction. "Residing in London." She tapped the leg of her quiet husband. "Mr. Fairchild, poor man. He has a gippy tummy. I insisted on visiting New York for our fiftieth wedding anniversary—I was born there—but it's changed so much, you see, I hardly recognised it. Made me nearly burst into tears. This trip has been such a frightful disappointment." She paused to catch her breath, then asked, "And you are?"

Ginger smiled. "I'm Mrs. Gold, and this ..."

Mrs. Fairchild's eyes darted to Haley, and she gasped with indignation. "You've brought your maid to breakfast?"

"No, no. This is my companion, Miss Higgins."

Haley, who was thumbing through Ginger's magazine, held it up to conceal herself and made a face. Ginger held in the giggle that threatened to burst forth. "She's a nurse."

"A nurse?" Mrs. Fairchild said. "Oh, well, that explains things, then."

"Miss Guilford would like honey, not jelly, and beef, not ham." The loud New Jersey accent of Nancy Guilford's assistant carried across the room and claimed the elder woman's attention.

A young waiter with hair as red as Ginger's said, "Will Miss Guilford be joining us soon, Miss Applebalm?"

"No. She has a headache and asked if I could bring breakfast up for her."

"Yes, miss."

Patty Applebalm's thin lips were pursed in determination. "And coffee, not tea. Miss Guilford doesn't like tea. And extra sugar if you don't mind."

"You and Nancy Guilford have something in common," Ginger said to Haley.

"Perhaps when it comes to coffee," Haley admitted, "but when it comes to clothes, she's all yours."

"I do adore her sense of fashion, though I think she's harder on her help than I am."

"Agreed," Haley said.

Ginger sighed. "I think I'll miss Molly."

"I'm sure she'll miss you too."

Ginger and Haley remained transfixed by the actress's assistant. "What do you think of Miss Applebalm?" Ginger asked.

"Do you mean, is she devoted or disgruntled?"

"Yes."

Haley thought for a moment, then answered, "I'd say devoted."

"I'd have to concur," Ginger said. "She has a bulldog intent on meeting Miss Guilford's requests, and when she looks at Nancy, I swear she appears sentimental."

Haley nodded. "I noticed that too. Perhaps Miss Applebalm is more than a simple hire."

"History between them?" Ginger asked.

"That's my guess."

"Aunt?"

"Possibly."

"I'm going to say she's Miss Guilford's aunt," Ginger said confidently. "One orphaned, one childless. Raised Nancy Guilford as her own."

"That's quite the guesswork," Haley replied.

"It's what I do when I'm bored."

Mrs. Fairchild leaned towards them, her bosom sprinkled with crumbs. "You're quite right, Mrs. Gold. I knew the Applebalms in the old days, poor as dirt. Young Nancy's mama died when she was little, and with no papa, her aunt, Miss Applebalm, loved her like she was her own. Would do anything for that girl, I reckon, anything."

Ginger found the quality of the older woman's hearing surprising and unnerving. She must remember to lower her voice in the future. She pushed away from the table and whispered to Haley, "I should go see to Boss. It's time for a trip to the kennel." Though Ginger managed to get around the rules about leaving her dog there, he still needed an opportunity to "do his business."

She spoke kindly to the Fairchilds before departing. "Good day. It was a pleasure to meet you."

* * *

Instead of heading immediately down to steerage, Ginger coaxed Boss up to the bridge deck that availed the best view. Pausing to enjoy the sunshine, Ginger leaned over the smoothly polished mahogany railing and watched the white swathe of waves that broke off the hull of the SS *Rosa* as she cut her path through the Atlantic.

The late-summer sun glinted off the sea, a glittering expanse as far as the eye could see, and a strong breeze fluttered the skirt of Ginger's blue dress around her calves. She used her free hand to hold on to her straw sunhat while tipping back her head to look up at the towering black and red painted smokestacks in the centre of the ship. They were even more impressive up close.

"I'll have you arrested for insubordination!"

Ginger recognised the angry voice and turned in time to see the captain and Chief Officer MacIntosh broach the top of the stairs on their way to the bridge.

"You rotten bounder!" MacIntosh shouted, traipsing a few steps behind.

Captain Walsh spun on his heel and jabbed MacIntosh in the chest. "You'll be lucky to get a job as a bloody seaman after I've finished with you."

They'd been so consumed with their argument they hadn't noticed Ginger standing there.

That was until Boss, noting the tension, barked. Ginger scolded herself for not giving her pet the sign to keep quiet.

The captain's and the chief officer's attention turned to Ginger.

"Oh, hello," Ginger called in an overly loud voice. "I didn't hear you there. I hope you don't mind that I came up to enjoy the view. Such a lovely day, isn't it? I'm sorry I can't stay longer, but I have to return my pup to the kennel. I know, I know, I'm not supposed to remove him from steerage, but I have a tendency to get my own way." She smiled widely and batted her eyes. "Please don't be angry with the boys in charge."

Captain Walsh relaxed into his professional demeanour and smiled as he approached. "Of course, Mrs. Gold, you are welcome to the entire ship. And we will ignore the kennel boys their indiscretion this once."

"Thank you," Ginger said, tugging on Boss's leash.

"Do enjoy the lovely weather," Captain Walsh said. "I'm afraid we're in for a change before we reach England."

"Oh? Nothing serious, I hope?" Ginger's stomach clenched at the thought of severe weather striking the SS *Rosa* mid-journey.

Captain Walsh responded with reassurance. "We'll be fine."

"Very well. Good day, Captain!" She looked for the

chief officer to offer a polite salutation, but he was no longer there.

Ginger found herself speed-walking down the decks to steerage. The argument she'd witnessed, and her subsequent performance, caused her heart to race. Before she reached the lower level and had to talk to the seaman who monitored all who came and went, she stopped to gain her composure.

Five years out of operations had made her soft.

CHAPTER FOUR

Boss whimpered, and Ginger knew she'd better get him to the kennel before he had an accident. When she reached the entrance to steerage, a different seaman from the day previous said, "Can I assist?"

Ginger patted the tips of her bobbed hair with her gloved hand. "I have special permission to bring my puppy in and out of the kennel. My name is Mrs. Gold. You can confirm with the captain." At least, this time the statement was true.

"Not necessary, madam. Your word is all I need."

Ginger braced herself for the change of atmosphere and descended. Located in the belly of the ship, the steerage was dark and smelly, not entirely due to the animals that resided there—the stench of human uncleanliness permeated the place as well. She was loath to spend too much time there for fear of bringing the smell back to first class.

She hated how snobbish that sounded, even to her. Third-class patrons stared unabashedly, and though Ginger did her best to dress simply, wearing her plainest frock and straw hat, there was no escaping that she came from privilege. The folks here wore worn, unfashionable clothes in bland colours. The women kept their hair in large, dull, tangled buns on the tops of their heads. The men's hair was longer than what was fashionable, and greasy without the aid of hair cream. The children ran around in bare feet. Wanting to appear friendly, Ginger tried smiling, but the women only frowned and pushed their children behind their backs, as if Ginger might be there to snatch them away.

Along with the dog kennel, other animals were stored there, mostly chickens and some piglets. There were even some cats, but Ginger imagined they lived on the ship to keep the rodent population down.

Ginger placed Boss on the ground, and said in greeting, "Hello, Scout." She'd learned the waif's name the day before and that he was an English orphan stowed onboard by one of the bellboys, his cousin Marvin.

"'Ello, miss." Scout kneeled, his scratched-up bare knee against the dusty wooden floor. "'ello, Boss, me mate. 'Ave to widdle, do ya?" Ginger handed over Boss's leash, and Scout disappeared with him. She wondered about the boy. Beneath the dirt on his face, the youngster's eyes were bright with optimism, his eager smile always at the ready. She was moved with a desire to help the lad, and perhaps he could be of help to her.

By the time he returned with a happy and much-relieved terrier, Ginger's plan was formulated.

"'Ere you go, miss," Scout said. "Boss did great." He flashed his large, toothy smile.

Ginger suppressed a giggle. "Understood."

Scout stared at her as she stood there, probably wondering why she hadn't skedaddled up the stairs the way she did last time. She hurried to relay her proposition.

"I'm in need of some help, Scout, and you look like the honest sort."

"Oh, I am, miss. Me mam taught me manners 'fore she died. And virtues, ma'am. Like 'onesty."

"Your mother sounds like she was a wonderful lady."

"She were, miss."

"I want to hire you to help me with Boss. He needs more fresh air and exercise than I'm able to give him." This was partially true. Though Ginger had time to walk him, Boss's presence in first class was deeply frowned upon and was prohibited at all the social events she planned to attend. She felt guilty about leaving him alone in her room so often.

"Yes, miss. I'd be 'appy to 'elp, but the guards at the door wun let me up."

"You let me worry about that. To be clear, this is a job, not a favour. I'll pay you three shillings for the duration of the trip."

Scout's young eyes lit up. "I'm yer man, miss."

Ginger fought the grin threatening to burst through. "I thought so. You have to be discreet, as other passengers with dogs aren't...bending the rules so much as I..."

"I is a ghost, miss. Practically invisible. And I know this ship like me own 'and, even the guard man dun know how much I know. There's plenty of places to take Boss where we won't bump into the likes of..."

Scout blushed, as if worried he might've offended Ginger by pointing out her class. She hurried to allay his fears.

"Exactly." She winked and handed him the coins. "No one in first class should even know Boss exists. Why don't you take Boss now? And I'll meet you on the second-class deck behind the engine room in an hour."

Scout reclaimed Boss's leash. "I just need to tell me cousin."

Ginger patted Boss's head. "You be a good boy. See you soon."

Ginger watched the interaction between the taller lad—lanky, with broad shoulders and a dark patch on his chin—and his young cousin. Marvin examined the coins and nodded his approval. Satisfied, Ginger ascended and made a deal with the seaman—it was amazing what a few bob would get you. When she reached the open deck, she took a long breath of the fresh sea air to cleanse her lungs.

Putting her self-professed sleuthing skills to work, she followed Scout and Boss, careful to remain a good distance back and out of sight. Scout did exactly as he promised, kept to second class in crannies and back areas reserved for storage. His kindness to Boss extended to the times when he didn't know he was being observed, which came as a huge relief to Ginger. In exactly an hour, thanks to a pocket watch Scout possessed, they showed up at the engine room door where Ginger arrived only minutes before.

"How did it go?" Ginger asked, scooping Boss into her arms.

"Jus' fine, miss. Me and Boss are chums."

"Indeed, you are." Satisfied by Scout's character, she kept him in mind should she need him for another job in the future.

CHAPTER FIVE

On the second night, the ship's crew planned a special cocktail-and-mingle event. Ginger held up a silk sea-green sleeveless gown with satin shoulder straps to her neck and then a gown in sapphire blue with sheer mid-length sleeves. The fabric of both dresses rippled just above Ginger's ankles. She chose the green to match her eyes, draping long loops of pearl beads around her neck. She added a matching headband with a large, dark feather pinned to the right side near her temple.

Haley wasn't as excited and steadfastly declined any offers of dress loans from Ginger. "I'd probably spill something on it."

"I doubt that," Ginger replied. "You have the steady hands of a surgeon."

"I'll just wear my suit," Haley insisted. "Or maybe, I'll stay here and keep *the boss* company."

Boss popped his head up upon hearing a version of his name.

"Nonsense!" Ginger made another effort and held out a simple pale-peach frock. "How about this? It's a lovely colour for you. It'll bring out the golden highlights in your beautiful chestnut hair. In fact, you can keep it. I never wear it anyway."

"I don't need your castoffs. And I don't have 'golden' highlights."

Ginger cocked a well-plucked brow. "I beg to differ."

"Fine." Haley snatched the dress from Ginger's hand. "But I'm not wearing"—she waved at Ginger's prominent feather—"*that*."

Ginger, feeling she'd won a small victory, said nothing. She sat at the dressing table and applied her makeup: smoky eye shadow reaching well-defined slender eyebrows, two applications of mascara, round spots of rouge under each high cheekbone, followed by a layer of mandarin-orange lipstick. She held a tissue to her mouth and pressed her lips against it.

Ginger considered Haley's reflection. She had an uncommonly wide jaw, but it was balanced out with a full mouth and lips. Her eyes were dark and shrouded with a sense of mystery. Somehow it all worked together and what should be a plain face was rather pleasant. With a bit of makeup, she could be striking.

"I could teach you."

"Teach me what?" Haley said.

"How to put on makeup." Ginger swivelled to face her. "Darling, it's easy and, well, you are rather pale."

Haley waved a hand in front of her face. "This is how the good Lord made me. Folks can take it or leave it."

Ginger grinned. She gave her friend credit for her aplomb.

***

Several electrical chandeliers lit up the cocktail lounge, its magical effect inducing a skip to Ginger's step. She loved parties and entertainment. A light chatter emanated from the populated tables amidst the melodic background music produced by a proficient pianist in the corner. She approached the bar with Haley at her side.

"The captain and Mrs. Walsh are here," Haley whispered.

"I was sure they would be," Ginger replied before approaching the couple. "Captain, Mrs. Walsh! How are you?"

The captain grasped Ginger's hand with both of his, perhaps holding on a mite too long. Ginger pulled away and extended her greeting to Mrs. Walsh, whose grasp was far less eager. Haley followed suit, and Ginger noted that the captain only gave her a quick single-handed shake.

"Quite well," Captain Walsh responded. "And you? I hope you are enjoying your journey so far?"

"Indeed. It's been entirely pleasant."

"What would you like from the bar?" he asked.

Ginger expressed a desire for a Mary Pickford, and Haley asked for a Sidecar—American cocktails—but fortunately, the waiter hailed from Boston and had likely learned of them as Ginger and Haley had, by visiting illegal speakeasies.

Ginger wasn't the kind who made a habit of breaking the law, but Haley dragged her out for a night of dancing and frivolity six months after her father had died. "You need to do something fun, Ginger. Your father wouldn't want you pouting about like this."

Haley was right about Ginger's father and about how much Ginger liked to have fun, and "speakeasy night" became a regular weekly outing. Their clandestine efforts, sneaking through dark streets, avoiding beat cops, and tapping on basement doors with a secret knock, provided a similar sort of emotional rush her work in the war had given her, with the bonus of it not being a matter of life and death or national security!

When Captain Walsh waved the waiter over to order for them, Ginger glimpsed the captain's polished gold cuff links, which sparkled in the glimmering light of the chandeliers.

"You've a nice selection of cuff links, Captain. I noticed the silver ones from yesterday with the fleur-de-lis."

The captain frowned. "Yes, those are a favourite of mine, sentimental reasons, but sadly, they've disappeared."

"Disappeared? As in you misplaced them, or were they...stolen?"

"I can't be certain, but, I hate to say it, I fear the latter."

"Perhaps I can help to find them." Ginger perked up at the thought. "I'm quite the finder of things, you know. My stepmother constantly loses miscellaneous items, which I manage to find. Once my father had a valuable piece go missing from his office and I tracked down the culprit, a devious member of our household staff."

The captain grinned, apparently enjoying Ginger's bright and positive attitude. "If you could acquire my missing possession, I would indeed be grateful, but please know that I shan't be disappointed if your pursuit is unfruitful. I rather expect they'll soon be melted down and sold."

Ginger smiled and sipped on her drink, enjoying the tangy rum and pineapple juice blend.

Haley nudged Ginger gently and whispered, "Two o'clock."

Ginger glanced to her right in time to spot Mrs.

Fairchild waddling towards them with a reluctant Mr. Fairchild.

"Hello, Mrs. Gold, Miss Higgins!"

Ginger and Haley greeted the couple.

"Are you going to delight us with a dance tonight?" Ginger asked.

"Oh, goodness gracious, no. We've no mind for this distasteful music." She winked. "We're here for the alcohol. We've three weeks of Prohibition to make up for!"

Ginger lifted her glass, "Quite right."

"Oh, but the ball, that's another story," Mrs. Fairchild said after ordering chardonnay for herself and whisky for her husband. "For that, we'll dance all night long. Waltzing is what I'd call real dancing. It's planned for the last night, did you know? By the way, I simply adore your gown. Did you get it in New York? They must import from Paris."

"They do, indeed, and yes, I bought this on Fifth Avenue."

Nancy Guilford arrived fashionably late, wearing a ruby-red cocktail dress with long beaded tassels, and a white feather boa draped over one shoulder. A shiny red headband encircled her blonde bob, which also sported a large feather, white to Ginger's black. Ginger felt a wave of irritation at being out-dressed by the woman.

The actress slinked past Ginger and Haley with barely a glance, her attention set firmly on the captain. The man nodded subtly, some kind of secret message? But not so subtly that Mrs. Walsh hadn't seen it. The frown on her already churlish expression deepened.

Ginger's attention was brought back from Mrs. Walsh by a jazz band setting up to replace the pianist, who promptly made his way to the bar and ordered a beer. Some of the tables were moved to the side to broaden the dance floor. Soon, the energetic music began, and enthusiastic dancers hopped to their feet.

The captain's interest in Ginger made her feel uneasy. Every time she'd glance his way, she found he was already staring at her.

Haley was right about him. He certainly wasn't showing respect to his wife by his blatant staring. In fact, she feared he was about to ask her to dance. To divert a possible awkward moment, Ginger took the offensive.

"Don't you just love this new jazz music, Mrs. Walsh? It's such fun!" The woman's expression was one of horror, but Ginger ignored her and turned to the captain before she could respond. "Captain Walsh, you should ask your wife to dance! Wouldn't we love to watch them, Haley?"

Haley looked surprised by Ginger's interference, but answered with a straight face. "I can think of nothing more enjoyable."

Captain Walsh's eyes flashed with confusion. He was one who had the utmost authority onboard and who was used to being thoroughly in control, and Ginger had shifted his footing. He cleared his throat and stood.

"I'm afraid I'm needed on the bridge." He put on his captain's hat. "Ladies."

Mrs. Walsh, apparently not wanting to remain in Ginger and Haley's company, excused herself immediately afterwards.

Haley muttered quietly, "Smooth work."

"I feared he was going to embarrass his wife by asking me to dance."

Ginger and Haley positioned themselves on high stools and observed the dance floor. As expected, Miss Guilford was continually engaged, gentlemen practically lining up and panting to dance with her. Poor Patty Applebalm was left alone at the table to guard Nancy Guilford's belongings. Next to the actress, Patty, with lines deepening around her eyes and mouth, sat in her simple blue gown. A wilting wallflower, indeed.

Ginger regarded the dapper gentleman from the evening before, whose eyes, like all the other men's eyes, were on Nancy Guilford. When the song ended and Miss Guilford returned to her table with a flourish, the man sauntered over.

Haley saw him too. "All men are alike," she said with reproach.

Then the dapper man surprised them both. Instead of asking Nancy Guilford to dance, he asked poor Patty!

"I recant what I just said," Haley murmured. "There's still a good one left."

Even more than Patty's shock and joy at the man's offer, Ginger enjoyed the expression of dismay and incomprehension on the actress's perfect face.

The dance ended, and Ginger ordered another drink. This time she chose a nice 1911 Clicquot champagne. "Why not?" she said with flair. "I paid full fare."

"Make sure you drink a glass of water too," Haley said. "And you are going to dance tonight, aren't you?"

"Why would you say that? I'm happy to listen and tap my feet."

"Because of *him*."

Ginger swung around to see the dapper gentleman heading towards them. She admired the way his soft summer-linen suit fit his six-foot frame. His slicked-back hair was well-styled, parted on the side and trimmed neatly around shapely ears. Only a hint of grey at his temples and a few lines fanning from his hazel eyes suggested his age.

"If you don't mind," Haley said, leaving quickly. "I have to use the convenience."

Before Ginger could stop her friend, the gentleman stood before her, offering his hand. "Would you like to dance?"

He spoke with a strong, clear English accent, and Ginger couldn't resist his charm. She lifted her gloved hand to accept his. "Certainly."

Up close, Ginger noted how the golden threads woven into his snappy blue tie brought out the gold flecks in his hazel eyes—intelligent eyes—which regarded her warmly.

"I suppose an introduction is in order," the man said as he spun her around the dance floor. "I'm Basil Reed."

"Mr. Reed, I'm Mrs. Gold." Ginger smiled up at him as she said it, but she wanted to be clear that she wasn't interested in a mid-Atlantic fling.

The music was too loud for them to converse, and the beat kept their feet moving. Ginger broke into the Charleston, her legs kicking at the knee ahead and behind, her arms swinging in time. Her pearl necklace jumped across her chest.

Basil Reed turned out to be a worthy partner, matching her beat for beat, his leather-bottomed shoes sliding expertly along the floor. Fashionable argyle socks peeked out from under the hem of his trousers.

"Thank you, Mr. Reed," she said with a smile as the man walked her back to her seat. "That was great fun!"

He removed a cotton handkerchief from his suit jacket and mopped his brow as he smiled at her. "The pleasure was all mine."

"I must start taking Boss out on longer walks," Ginger said, her hand to her chest as she caught her breath.

Basil Reed arched a brow. "You take your boss for walks? What on earth is it that you do?"

"No, no," Ginger said, laughing. "Boss is my dog. He's a Boston terrier, you see. Boss is short for Boston, and as my friend Miss Higgins insists, he does think he's the boss."

"I take it he's in the kennel."

Ginger replied without hesitation, "Of course."

At the bar, Ginger said, "It was nice to meet you, Mr. Reed." Ginger returned to her seat next to where Haley sat waiting, and Basil Reed sauntered back to his table on the other side of the room.

"*So?*" Haley said, with an exaggerated wink.

Ginger pretended not to notice. "So what?"

Before Haley could prod deeper, Ginger's attention was directed elsewhere. Nancy Guilford was having words with the captain who'd returned from the bridge. Ginger couldn't hear what was said, but the cross look on the actress's face proved the conversation wasn't pleasant. The captain spun on his heels, spurning her. Her face flushed as red as her cocktail dress, and she flung her champagne flute to the floor where it shattered to pieces.

The captain shot her a disapproving look over his shoulder but kept his stride. Realising the attention of the room was on her, Nancy waved her arms dramatically and pouted. "I'm so clumsy!"

The redheaded waiter rushed to sweep the glass and mop up.

"Such a waste," Ginger said.

"Of time?" Haley said dryly.

"Of good champagne."

CHAPTER SIX

The next day as Ginger slept through breakfast, she admitted to herself that perhaps she'd had a little bit too much to drink the night before. Haley brought her coffee and dry toast, and by noon she was feeling well enough to take part in the luncheon.

When she got to the dining room, she casually glanced around and noticed a few familiar faces. Nancy Guilford made a personal appearance sitting with Patty Applebalm, who wore a gingham day dress and low-heeled oxfords, quite suitable for the time of day and her station. The actress, though, in Ginger's opinion, was overdressed for luncheon. She wore a long frock with her trademark calf slits, and her face was laden with makeup. It was almost like she'd slept in her evening wear the night before and only recently woken. Perhaps she had. On closer inspection, the makeup did appear smudged. Patty reached over to wipe a spot of egg from the corner of Nancy's mouth, an act of kindness Nancy didn't appreciate, and she smacked away the older woman's hand.

Mr. Basil Reed caught Ginger's eye as she and Haley strode across the room. Haley noticed the exchange.

"He's attractive," she said as they selected a table.

Ginger sat gracefully in the seat opposite her. "He's too old for me."

Haley huffed. "Your father married a younger woman."

"Look how that turned out."

"It turned out well for her."

"I suppose. But my father was rich. She'd never have married him otherwise."

"Are you saying you're not interested in Mr. Reed because he's not rich enough? Surely he must have some money to afford first class."

"Of course not. Mr. Reed's financial status is of no concern to me. *You* know the reason I'm not interested."

Mentioning the man's name had conjured him. "Ladies, may I join you?"

Ginger blinked back a wave of embarrassment. Had Mr. Reed heard them talk about him? And worse, how had she grown so careless as to be caught out like that? She was normally very astute. She promptly recovered.

"Please do. In fact, we were just talking about you."

Basil Reed occupied the chair nearest Ginger and raised a dark brow. "Is that so?"

"Yes, Miss Higgins was saying how she wished she had danced at the cocktail party."

Haley shot her a dirty look.

Basil smiled at Haley. "I don't believe we've been formally introduced." He removed his hat and stretched out an arm. "I'm Basil Reed. And I apologise for being amiss last night. My manners were dreadful, but I confess, I don't remember seeing you there."

"Miss Higgins," Haley said. "And please, don't mind Mrs. Gold's mistaken inference."

"Miss Higgins is a nurse," Ginger said. "She cared for my father before he passed away last year, and we became dear friends over that sad time."

Basil Reed held Ginger's gaze and added politely, "I'm sorry to hear about your father."

Haley turned her attention to the day's menu. "I hope you like onions, Mr. Reed," she said. "The entrée is French onion soup."

"One of my favourite soups, Miss Higgins."

The food arrived courtesy of the redheaded waiter who had served Ginger before. He wore a name tag—Roy Hardy—and the buoyant smile of someone who loved their job.

"Thank you, Mr. Hardy," Ginger said as the server placed the meal on the table.

"You're welcome, Mrs. Gold. Enjoy."

Ginger and Haley removed their gloves before beginning the entrée—which, along with slices of fresh-baked baguette, was simply delicious. They made light discussion with Mr. Reed about the differences between American and English social customs and the bright future ahead for both nations.

"Certainly, housewives have benefited from kitchen items like electric mixers for baking, and vacuum cleaners for simpler housework," Ginger remarked.

Basil Reed looked at her as if he didn't quite understand, and then said, "Oh, you mean Hoovers."

"Tomato, tom*ah*to," Haley murmured between sips.

"Also the automobile industry," Basil Reed added. "Thanks to, for the most part, your own Henry Ford."

Haley nodded. "Good old Henry."

"Who would've guessed that every home could soon be

in possession of a radio," Ginger said. "So essential for the growth of culture."

"And the delivery of information," Basil said. "Like politics."

Ginger stared at him. "Indeed."

The main course of moist baked halibut dressed in a creamy lemon and basil sauce with a side of buttery green beans arrived.

"Smells scrumptious!" Ginger said. "Monsieur Babineaux is a charm! The French seem to enter the world possessing exceptional culinary talent."

Once they all sampled their first bites and made appropriate yet subtle noises of approval, Ginger turned to Basil Reed. "Mr. Reed, do tell us a bit about yourself. Were you born and raised in London?"

"Yes, madam." He gestured with his left hand. "I know London inside and out."

Ginger had noticed the plain gold band on the man's ring finger the evening before. Had he, too, suffered the loss of a spouse?

"Is there a Mrs. Reed?"

A shadow crossed their companion's face for an instant. "Yes."

"She didn't join you on your trip to America?" Haley said. "I hope she's not in ill health." Haley poised herself like she was just being a concerned nurse and doctor in training, but Ginger knew Haley's curiosity was more personal.

Basil Reed hesitated. "Unfortunately, Mrs. Reed is visiting her sister in Paris." He adeptly changed the subject. "Miss Higgins, what brings you to London?"

"I'm studying to become a medical doctor."

"That's quite, um, ambitious."

Haley leaned back and crossed her arms. "For a woman?"

Ginger bit back a grin. Haley was about to launch into her views on feminism.

"Mr. Reed," Haley continued with a clipped voice. "All women in America now have the right to vote, not just those who are over thirty, like in your country. American women are considered equals to their male counterparts. Any profession that a man may pursue is available to a woman, and if it is not, it damn well should be."

Basil Reed sat back as if he'd been attacked by a gale wind. "My apologies, Miss Higgins. I never meant to offend. I'm sure ladies everywhere would appreciate having more female doctors about. And, of course, I support women's right to vote. I do hope that the British Parliament will soon pass a law to match the forward thinking that is found in America."

Basil Reed took a long sip of his coffee and shifted his focus to Ginger. "How about you? What brings you to London? Are you on holiday?" He glanced at her ring finger and threw the question back. "Without your husband?"

"Sadly, my husband passed in the war."

Basil Reed twitched at his unintentional insensitivity. "My condolences."

"It's quite all right, Mr. Reed. My trip to London is more business than pleasure. I must attend to my father's estate. It was serendipitous that Miss Higgins was heading there at the same time. Once the matter has been sorted, I'll be returning to Boston."

"Your father was English, then?"

"Oh, yes, through and through. Right up to teatime at four p.m. with crustless cucumber sandwiches and beans on his breakfast toast."

"He sounds delightful." Basil Reed considered her. "It makes sense now how an American woman could come across so English."

"Yes, I adore the benefits found in both cultures."

"Righto. Well, I do hope that you enjoy London for as long as you might stay."

The waiter returned to retrieve the dirty dishes, and Haley stood. "It's been a pleasure, Mr. Reed," she said, "but you must excuse me. I need to return to my books."

Basil Reed looked perplexed as he watched her go. "Your friend's the serious type, isn't she?"

Ginger laughed. "You could say that."

Haley wasn't gone long before their attention was captured by a loud commotion coming from the kitchen.

"What do you suppose is going on in there?" Ginger said.

Basil Reed wiped his mouth with a cloth serviette. "Your guess is as good as mine."

Babineaux rushed across the dining room to Mrs. Walsh's table. He spoke too softly into her ear for Ginger to understand what he said, but the expression on Mrs. Walsh's face was of shock and horror.

Nancy Guilford, whose gaze scanned the room nonstop —no doubt searching for the captain—approached Mrs. Walsh's table unabashedly.

"What's the matter, puddin'?" she asked with her nasal voice. "Has something happened?"

Mrs. Walsh turned away, and much to Miss Guilford's chagrin, Babineaux took the actress's elbow and guided her back to her own table.

"Please excuse me," Ginger said, leaving to see to Mrs. Walsh before Mr. Reed could say anything to stop her. She had a sinking feeling in her stomach as she approached the woman.

"Is something wrong, Mrs. Walsh? Anything I can help you with?"

Mrs. Walsh covered her mouth with her fingers, pushed away from her table, and rushed out of the room. Ginger stared after her.

Babineaux returned and said with a thick French accent, "*Eet ees* terrible, madame."

"What's happened, Monsieur Babineaux?"

Babineaux's voice wavered. "I am so sorry to have to tell you that Captain Walsh *ees* dead."

CHAPTER SEVEN

Ginger sensed Basil Reed approaching from behind.

"I'm Chief Chief Inspector Reed from the London Crime Investigations Division. Is there a matter here that I can assist with?"

Ginger swivelled on her heels and raised a questioning brow. "Mr. Reed, such a secret to keep up your sleeve."

"I do apologise, Mrs. Gold, but my occupation seemed irrelevant until now."

"I suppose I'll have to get used to calling you Chief Inspector."

"Is there a problem at hand?" Basil Reed repeated. The query was a courtesy. Chief Chief Inspector Reed stared at Ginger and Babineaux in turn with a look of determination. He wore his title with authority, and there was no question that he intended to take charge of the situation.

"*Mon Dieu,*" Babineaux said. He spoke into the chief inspector's ear and Chief Inspector Reed frowned.

"Please lead me to the scene."

When it became apparent that Ginger was following,

Chief Inspector Reed stopped her. "Mrs. Gold, I do believe this is a matter for the police, and I imagine, quite delicate."

"I'm not as sensitive as I may appear, *Chief Inspector*," Ginger returned. "Captain Walsh was a family friend. I insist that you allow me to accompany you."

The chief inspector stared at Ginger with a flash of perplexity, as if he wasn't entirely certain as to what to do with Ginger's adamant outburst, but he apparently came to the conclusion that it wasn't a good time or place to argue. As they followed Babineaux through the kitchen, Ginger pulled Roy Hardy aside.

"Please summon Miss Higgins in Room 45 and tell her to come to the the restaurant. Tell her to ask for me. It's of the utmost importance." She slipped five shillings into the waiter's hand, and he took off at a jog.

Ginger ensured that members of the kitchen staff saw her traipse after the cook, and caught up to Chief Inspector Reed and Babineaux just as they started to descend a long, circular staircase and into the belly of the ship.

"Where are we going, Mr. Babineaux?" the chief inspector asked.

"New supplies were loaded up in Boston. I always oversee the menus and monitor that we have enough of what *ees* needed each day. There *ees* a dry pantry and a cool pantry, with ice," he added with a tinge of pride in his voice.

Ginger thought that made good sense and knew how much their cook back in Boston appreciated their new refrigerator.

Babineaux yanked on a heavy wooden door, and they were hit with a waft of cold air. A contrast to Ginger's warm skin, the chill caused her to shiver. The walls were lined with shelving, half-empty now due to the fact they were beyond the midpoint of their voyage. The interior smelled musty, of old vegetables, and slightly sour, like brine. A row of large oak barrels stood along the back wall.

"Mrs. Gold?" Haley's voice echoed down the stairwell.

"Down here, Miss Higgins," Ginger said.

Haley appeared and tried to make sense of the situation. "What, dare I ask, is going on?"

"Our poor captain has been killed," Ginger said. "Monsieur Babineaux just made the grisly discovery."

"His body was found down here?" Haley asked.

Babineaux answered, "Yes, *meess*."

Haley frowned. "How odd."

"Mrs. Gold," Chief Inspector Reed said. "I must object!"

"Nurse Higgins served in the war," Ginger said with a dismissive wave. "I'm quite certain she's seen far worse than she'll see today. Her medical experience might come in handy, might it not?"

Haley didn't wait for Basil Reed to answer and asked Ginger, "Why is he here?"

"Because, Miss Higgins, our dear Mr. Reed is also known in London as Chief Chief Inspector Reed."

Haley stared at Basil Reed. "Indeed?"

"Yes, indeed," Chief Inspector Reed said, losing patience. "Now, Mr. Babineaux, if you'd be so kind as to lead us to the body."

Ginger began to wonder about that as well. She'd scoured the cold room, the shelving and floor, and failed to spot the captain.

The cook stopped at an especially large barrel with the lid resting crookedly. That could account for the strong scent of brine.

"Please explain," the chief inspector said.

Babineaux cleared his throat. "This *ees* a pickle barrel.

Eet' ees almost empty, but I wanted to rescue the stragglers before opening the next one."

Ginger pulled a face. "Don't tell me the captain is in that barrel."

Babineaux's chin fell to his chest. "I am afraid so."

Chief Inspector Reed looked back at Ginger and Haley. "Do you still want to stay?"

Ginger nodded. She served in France during the war. Her stomach was strong.

"If you don't mind, sir," Haley said with renewed deference to Chief Inspector Reed. "I would appreciate the opportunity to assist with the examination."

"That would be up to the ship's doctor," Chief Inspector Reed said. "As for me, I have no issue with it."

Babineaux removed the lid, allowing first the chief inspector and then Ginger and Haley to peer in. Ginger grimaced at the sight of the bloated, pale body of her father's friend. *Oh, mercy.*

Chief Inspector Reed checked his wristwatch. "Thirty-two hours before we dock. It's not much time. Unless we find out who the killer is before then, no one will be disembarking when we get to Liverpool."

CHAPTER EIGHT

Ginger was morbidly fascinated by the corpse laid out on the makeshift table that had been brought into the cold pantry by two strong sailors.

The ship's physician, "Ol' Doc Johnson," was a man nearing his seventies with wisps of grey hair around his ears and sloping shoulders. He seemed flustered by the dramatic events.

"We've never had a murder onboard the *Rosa* before." A gnarled hand shook as he rubbed white whiskers on his chin. "Mainly headaches and colds and, of course, seasickness. Oh, there was that one bout of influenza, mind you, a particularly nasty business, but never a murder, no, never."

"It's kind of you to allow me to assist with the examination," Haley said. "It will help me as I further my studies." The old doc nodded, his face flushing crimson with apparent relief.

Ginger briefly considered returning to her room to retrieve a shawl in deference to the cold of the pantry, but the adrenaline burst she experienced as a result of this shocking event kept her sufficiently warm.

Introduction to medical jurisprudence was a subject of study for Ginger when she attended college. But that was over a decade ago and the field had certainly developed since. Once again, she found herself envying Haley, but resigned to her lot in life, finding some comfort in the idea that she could learn vicariously through her friend.

The cold pantry now virtually reeked of brine and something worse. Ginger held a cotton handkerchief to her nose. Chief Officer MacIntosh was informed of the captain's death and oversaw the undignified process of removing Captain Walsh's folded-up body, stiff with rigor mortis, from the barrel. The procedure took three seamen, a crowbar, and a mop.

Now the captain's body was curled up like an oversized fetus under a crisp sheet. His once-handsome face was bloated and a ghastly white, his lips a dreadful shade of blue.

Haley examined the corpse with professional efficiency, checking the fingernails, scalp, and skin surface for bruising.

"Well?" Ginger inquired.

Chief Inspector Reed cleared his throat as if to remind her who was in charge.

"There are two contusions on the back of his skull, a small one and a deeper one," Haley said. "However, the fluid released from his lungs smells strongly of brine, suggesting the cause of death as drowning rather than blunt force trauma, but an official autopsy would confirm."

"You mean to say the chap might've been alive when he was inserted into the pickle barrel?" Chief Inspector Reed asked.

Haley nodded. "It's possible, but with the head injury this severe, it's very likely he was unconscious. Also there are no splinters or wood fibres under his fingernails to indicate that he struggled inside of it."

"How long has he been dead?" Ginger asked, and again the chief inspector's handsome hazel eyes flashed with annoyance.

"Well, we know he was alive at dinner last night," Haley said. "According to the captain's watch, he was placed in the barrel at 2:34 a.m. But that doesn't tell me when the head trauma occurred. Lividity is apparent and starts at his waist." Haley folded the sheet down to the area where the deep purple of collected blood began. "This indicates he's been dead for at least six hours."

Ginger gave Chief Inspector Reed a pointed look as if to say, *I told you she was good*, then added, "I'd try to find out who saw him last and at what time."

As if he didn't appreciate being told how to do his job, the chief inspector's expression darkened with slight indignation. "Thank you, ladies for your help thus far. I've sent a telegram to Scotland Yard, and this case is now officially under my jurisdiction. I'm asking you to please leave the investigation to me from here on in."

"Of course," Ginger said. She smiled demurely at Chief Inspector Reed as he watched them leave. Once up the stairwell and out of earshot, she said, "We need to talk to Mrs. Walsh and Miss Guilford. The wife first, I think."

Haley stared firmly at Ginger. "Did you not just hear what the chief inspector said?"

"I did. He said not to *officially* investigate. Besides, I merely want to offer my condolences. Maybe we should bring a gift?"

"I don't believe there's a gift shop onboard."

"True. However, I do have a couple of bottles of Boston's best bootlegged brandy. I could offer her one."

Haley arched an eyebrow. "A whole bottle?"

"So right. She'll have glasses in her room as we do. We'll offer her a drink."

CHAPTER NINE

Along their passage through second class towards the stairwell that led to their deck, Ginger noticed their chambermaid, Chloe, refilling a linen cupboard. She was young, still in her teens, with creamy brown skin and shiny black hair tied neatly into a bun on the back of her head. Ginger guessed her to be of Spanish descent, with pretty brown eyes and a simpering smile that was sure to turn the heads of a lot of young men.

That included the one standing a yard away, removing folded linen tablecloths and serviettes. It was the redheaded Roy Hardy. The way he pretended not to notice Chloe made Ginger's heart melt.

Poor thing!

Chloe finally acknowledged his presence and smiled before walking away. Roy Hardy was so captivated that the linens in his arms slipped to the floor.

"Blimey!" he muttered as he knelt to pick them up.

Ginger tapped Haley's arm. "I'll meet you in the room."

"Playing cupid? Now? Really, Ginger, your timing."

"I'll just be a minute. The youth is in desperate need of heart assistance!"

Haley shook her head and kept walking.

Ginger turned to the waiter who was busy picking up the pile of fabric and refolding. "Hello, Mr. Hardy."

Roy Hardy's chin snapped up, and the red flush in his face grew even redder.

"Oh, Mrs. Gold. Please excuse me. I fumbled."

Ginger bent down to assist. "I quite understand. Miss Chloe is a beautiful girl."

Roy Hardy's eyes turned to saucers, and he looked mortified.

"It's all right," Ginger said quickly. "It's perfectly natural for a young man such as yourself to be interested in a young girl like Miss Chloe."

"Except she's beyond seeing anything worthwhile in me."

"Oh, come now. She's just as shy as you are. Have you spoken to her yet?"

"No, ma'am. I want to, but whenever I'm near her, my mind goes blank and my tongue dries like a leather knot." Roy returned the tablecloths to the closet. "I don't really need any linen, I just know she'll be here this time of day, and I make an excuse to come."

Ginger handed Roy her stack of newly folded serviettes. "You're putting in a good effort, and I'm certain it's not gone to waste. I may be able to be of some help to you, but I'm truly in a hurry right now. I'll find you later to discuss this further. Good day, Mr. Hardy."

Roy Hardy called after her. "Good day, Mrs. Gold. And thank you!"

Haley washed and changed her suit, which Ginger thought prudent after Haley's interaction with a corpse.

Ginger wished she could change as well, but they needed to hurry if they hoped to get to Mrs. Walsh before the chief inspector did. At best, she could put on clean gloves and add a shawl to stave off the chills that had beset her in the cold pantry once the novelty of viewing the crime scene wore off.

"Where's the boss?" Haley asked as she put on a pair of black wrist-length gloves.

"Young Scout from steerage has him this morning. Since I'm rather busy today, I sent a message for him to drop Boss off. I arranged for Miss Chloe to let Boss in the room if I happen to be out." Ginger opened one of her drawers and removed a twenty-five-ounce bottle of brandy. "Walking into a liquor store in London is going to feel so anticlimactic."

"Almost not worth doing," Haley said slyly.

Ginger scoffed. "I wouldn't go that far. Are you ready?"

"Lead the way."

* * *

Ginger knocked tentatively on Mrs. Walsh's door. "Mrs. Walsh, are you there?"

Silence. Ginger cast a glance at Haley. If Mrs. Walsh wasn't in her room, where was she?

She knocked again. "Mrs. Walsh? Are you all right?"

Finally, they heard the padding of soft footsteps towards the door and then the sound of the key in the lock.

"Mrs. Walsh," Ginger said kindly. "We're so sorry to intrude. Please allow us to offer our condolences." Ginger lifted up her offering. "I know it's early for spirits, but I thought under the circumstances..."

Mrs. Walsh eyed the bottle, then invited them in. "That

old codger, Dr. Johnson, gave me something for my nerves, but I don't think it's working." She sighed heavily. "This is just so bloody awful."

Haley collected three glasses that sat next to a crystal decanter and arranged them in front of the standard set of wax candles. Ginger poured, offering Mrs. Walsh the first glass. The woman accepted it with a shaky hand and took a big gulp.

"*Mon Dieu*, that's good." She settled down into one of the armchairs, which was upholstered in pink with fine gold embroidery woven throughout.

"You're French?" Ginger asked.

"*Oui*. Born in Calais, but immigrated to England when I met Mr. Walsh." As if her life was too sad to ponder, she sighed again, and took another drink.

Like the windows in the room Ginger and Haley shared, these smaller ones provided a nice view of the ocean. This room appeared larger, though, with just one double-sized bed. Ginger took a sip of brandy and claimed one of the empty chairs while Haley remained standing by the sideboard.

A quick inventory of the space revealed no immediate signs of a male presence—no men-sized shoes, or pipes and tobacco, or large overcoats.

"I'm so sorry this happened to you, Mrs. Walsh," Ginger said.

"Do call me Elise. I think we're beyond formalities now."

"Of course. And please call me Ginger."

Elise nodded grimly and took another sip.

"My father passed last year," Ginger said. "It was a horrible time in my life, so I can imagine how you might be feeling."

"My condolences," Elise Walsh said simply.

"Did you awaken at all when your husband left the room in the middle of the night? Did you notice the time?"

Elise Walsh scowled and spoke dryly, "I'm afraid that the captain and I sit together at mealtimes for the sake of appearances only. Mr. Walsh and I each have our own staterooms." She pointed to a closed door on the other side. "His room connects to mine through there."

Ginger suspected as much, and now she longed to get into that room to investigate. "I'm sorry," she said. "I didn't know."

"When was the last time you saw your husband alive?" Haley asked.

"Shortly after dinner yesterday." Her eyes welled up with tears. "Our marriage might not have been smooth sailing, but I still loved him. I can't believe I'm never going to see him again."

Despite the pun, Elise's grief seemed genuine. Though, Ginger supposed, a person could intentionally kill someone and then regret the act afterwards. Or be really good at acting.

"Did the captain have any enemies?"

"Why you are asking me these questions, Ginger," Mrs. Walsh snapped. "Isn't that the job of the police?"

Ginger was undaunted. "I confess, I've always been a curious sort. You could consider this practice for when the chief inspector does question you. Give you a chance to work out how to respond."

Elise Walsh stared hard as she considered Ginger's words, then relented. "Perhaps. Although I have nothing to hide."

Ginger tried again. "So, did he? Did Captain Walsh have enemies?"

"For the most part, Joseph was well-liked. I don't believe he had any real enemies. In fact, the opposite is true. Too many people loved him," she said with a note of bitterness.

"Are you referring to Miss Guilford?"

Elise Walsh sat up sharply. "You know about Nancy Guilford?"

"It's a presumption based on observation."

"Such a trollop!" Elise spat. "If a woman plans on cheating with another woman's husband, at the very least she should have the decency to be discreet."

So, Mrs. Walsh knew that her husband was unfaithful.

Elise threw back the final drop of brandy and held out her glass for a second round. Ginger poured, remembering how the captain had unceremoniously pointed out her drinking problem.

"I lied about Joseph not having enemies," Elise Walsh said after another gulp. "He had at least one."

"Oh?" Ginger prodded.

"He was being blackmailed."

CHAPTER TEN

The air seemed to vacate the room. A cloud mass suddenly shielded the sun, filling the space with an ominous shadow. Ginger and Haley shared a look of surprise before Ginger spoke.

"Who's been blackmailing him?"

"I have no idea," Elise Walsh answered coolly. "I only know because I discovered a letter in his jacket pocket."

As curious as Ginger was, she didn't feel it wise to ask Mrs. Walsh why she was fishing through her husband's pockets. "Do you know what the offence is? What did the blackmailer have on Captain Walsh?"

"I wish I knew. Now it's possible we'll never know." The pupils in Elise's grey eyes widened slightly, and the corner of her mouth twitched.

Mrs. Walsh was lying.

Elise lifted the near-empty glass to her lips and tipped her head back to finish it. "As you can imagine," she said, "this is all very taxing." She stood to make her point clear that she wanted them to leave.

Taking the hint, Ginger made sure to snag the half-empty bottle of brandy before saying her goodbyes to the new widow.

"So, what do you make of that?" Haley asked as she and Ginger headed down the exterior corridor to the port side of the ship where their room was located.

"I believe Mrs. Walsh was telling the truth about the blackmailing, but she was lying about not knowing the reasons why. Either way, it gives her a strong motive. Gain revenge on her cheating husband *and* break the powerful grip of the blackmailer."

"Although the blackmailer could simply turn his attention to her," Haley offered.

"Hmm." Ginger said. "Mrs. Walsh spoke as if that wasn't a possibility, which means she doesn't believe it will affect her."

"Except for her reputation."

"She might think it's gone already. It appears the captain wasn't very subtle about his affairs."

"It would be interesting to know whether the captain left her anything," Haley said.

"*Oh, mercy*," Ginger mused. "Perhaps he was about to change his will to favour someone else?"

"A mistress?"

"My guess would be the actress."

"Miss Guilford certainly didn't enjoy watching the captain dine with his wife," Haley said.

"Indeed not. Miss Guilford doesn't seem to be the type of lady who likes to play second fiddle, not even to the wife. It's clear from her performance in the cocktail lounge that she demands attention."

Ginger unlocked the door to their stateroom, and Boss hopped off his pillow to greet her.

"You're back!" Ginger swooped the small dog into her

arms, letting him kiss her face, and made a mental note to give Miss Chloe an extra tip when she saw her again. Thinking about the chambermaid reminded her of her promise to Mr. Hardy. She needed a way to have those two shy people speak together.

She put the pup down as she had yet to relieve herself of the brandy. He followed her about the room, stubby tail wagging. "Sorry we've been so long, Bossy," she sang. "Mama's got a murder to solve and it can't be helped."

Ginger removed her gloves, folded them, and placed them in one of the drawers, her mind back on the case. "Maybe the captain finally told Miss Guilford he was never going to leave his wife, so she decided to do away with him by hitting him on the head with a yet-unknown blunt object."

"That might be motive," Haley said as she sat at the table and opened her textbooks. "But she's not strong enough to lift him into a pickle barrel."

"She's not, but Officer MacIntosh is," Ginger said, taking a seat by the window. Boss took that as a sign to climb onto his mistress's lap. "You remember the argument I told you about, between him and the captain."

"I wish we knew what they were fighting over."

"As do I." Ginger crossed her legs, and Boss readjusted himself accordingly. "And this raises another question. If you were going to kill a man on a ship, would you hide his body in a pickle barrel?"

Haley shook her dark curls. "I'd push him overboard and not risk a body being found."

"Which means that whoever killed Captain Walsh wanted him to be found."

"Proof of death?"

"That sounds sinister."

Haley nodded. "Almost like organised crime or something."

Ginger stood and placed Boss back onto his pillow, and the dog spun in a tight circle before settling.

"Who else would have a motive and means to kill the captain?" Haley said.

Ginger paced the space between herself and Haley. "It could be anyone, really. It's not as if we know everyone onboard."

"That's true."

"But I can't stop thinking about how Babineaux and Mrs. Walsh look at each other. Seems to me they are more than just casual acquaintances."

"Do you think the cook killed the captain to gain the captain's wife?" Haley said. "He would be strong enough to put the body in the pickle barrel."

"Yes, but why would he then turn around and announce that it was there?"

"Perhaps Babineaux thought that 'finding' the body would keep him above suspicion."

"That still doesn't answer the question as to why he wouldn't just push the corpse overboard," Ginger said.

Haley concurred. "It doesn't."

"That makes Mrs. Walsh, Miss Guilford, Chief Officer MacIntosh, and Cook Babineaux all potential suspects."

"Who do we talk to next?" Haley asked.

"Good question." Ginger sat at the dressing table, ran a brush through her hair, and tidied her bob. "We mustn't get in the way of the chief inspector. We were lucky to get to Elise Walsh before he did, but we have to assume he has learned of the blackmail."

"The chief inspector does seem to be attentive and

attuned to his surroundings," Haley said with a wink. "He seems pretty attentive and attuned to you."

Ginger chuckled. "Stay on track, dear Nurse Higgins. Stay on track."

"If you insist," Haley said. "What's next? A visit to Miss Guilford?"

CHAPTER ELEVEN

Ginger hooked her arm through Haley's as she coached Boss along on a leash. She didn't want to leave him alone in their state room, and it was too inconvenient and time sensitive to seek out young Scout again.

They made their way to the concierge to inquire of Miss Guilford's room number. The concierge, a youth whose name tag read "Ernest," appeared besotted by Ginger's larger-than-life persona. Or perhaps he was just wary of the dog. It was hard to read the younger generation these days.

"Have you met my Boston terrier?" Ginger said, smiling brightly. "His name is Boss."

"No, madam. I haven't had the pleasure." Ernest knelt lower and stretched out a hand. "He's a friendly sort?"

"He just ate, so you should be fine."

Ernest snapped back his hand and stared at Ginger with a startled look.

"Oh, I'm just teasing you, Ernest. Boss is perfectly friendly."

Ernest let out a slow chuckle and made a second

attempt. Boss leaned into the young man's hand and relished the scratching behind his ear. His pink tongue licked the air with approval.

"Boss is supposed to stay in the kennel for the trip, but I just can't bear the thought of leaving him there. A little walk for fresh air must be okay."

"I'm a dog owner myself," Ernest said, shrugging. "German shepherd. Maxine."

"A lovely breed. So smart!"

"She is, madam. Smarter than a lot of blokes I know."

"I'm sure Maxine can't wait for you to get home." Ginger looked him in the eye. "Ernest? I'm wondering if you could help me out. We had the privilege of dining with Miss Nancy Guilford the other night," Ginger said, pouring on English charm. "Such a delightful woman, and we got on so splendidly. I simply must see her again before we disembark. I would hate for a potential friendship to be squandered. I'm just so sorry for not getting her telephone number. Silly me." Ginger batted her eyelashes at the enamoured young man.

Haley tried hard not to roll her eyes.

"It's against our policy to give out personal information on our passengers, but since we're docking soon, I don't see how it should be a problem." The concierge relinquished the room number. Miss Guilford's stateroom was located on the starboard side. It was on the same side as the Walshes, but nearer to the bow. Still plenty of opportunity for awkward encounters.

"Thank you, Ernest!" Ginger blew him a kiss. "You're such a peach."

"And you are shameful," Haley said under her breath as they walked away.

"Yet I got the room number, didn't I?"

"For that, I say, well done. How, exactly, do you plan to present us to Miss Guilford?" Haley said. "I doubt she even knows we exist."

"I doubt she knows anyone exists who is not in her entourage," Ginger replied. "Film stars live in their own fantasy world."

"I hear she's going to be in a talkie next," Haley said.

"With that voice?"

Ginger and Haley turned onto the corridor where Nancy Guilford's room was situated, just as the door of the room in question opened and Chief Officer MacIntosh slipped out. Ginger and Haley ducked back behind the corner before he could see them. Ginger held her finger to her lips for Boss' sake.

"That's interesting," she said once MacIntosh was out of sight.

"Very interesting, indeed," Haley said. "Nancy Guilford and the first officer are acquainted. Lovers?"

"Coconspirators to murder?"

"What could possibly be their motives?"

"Perhaps the chief officer would like to be captain one day."

"You think he'd kill for that?" Haley said.

"I don't know," Ginger said. "What else would he have to gain?"

"Maybe he was the blackmailer, and after demanding more money, he and the captain got into a fight," Haley said. "In a rage, MacIntosh killed him."

"It's possible, and it could very well be what they were arguing about. Or it's possible it's purely greed for power. MacIntosh is now the standing captain for the duration of this trip. We need to find out whether he would remain the captain of this vessel indefinitely."

"His motive could be as simple as a lover's quarrel," Haley said. "Perhaps MacIntosh, besotted now with the sensual Miss Guilford, fell into a jealous rage with the prospect of sharing her."

"The argument between the men could've been over Miss Guilford then," Ginger said.

"MacIntosh's definitely strong enough to put a man into a barrel."

Haley slowed as they reached Miss Guilford's door. "But that still leaves the question as to why bother."

"A body would be preserved in pickle juice somewhat, wouldn't it?" Ginger asked.

Haley conceded. "Perhaps for a very short while."

"But long enough to get it to shore tomorrow night, surely?"

"Yes. That raises the question as to why the killer wants to preserve the body. Is it more than just proof of death? If not, what does our killer need to prove?"

Ginger knocked. Unlike Mrs. Walsh's slow response, the door opened immediately. The smile on Nancy Guilford's face dropped when she saw who it was.

"Were you expecting someone else?" Ginger asked.

The actress sneered and said with her nasal drawl, "Wasn't expecting you, Mrs. Gold."

"So, you do know who I am."

"The captain liked to rave about you and his connection to your family." She squinted suspiciously. "Why are you here?"

Ginger dug into her shoulder bag and produced the half bottle of brandy. At this rate, if they drank with every suspect they queried, they were going to be sloshed by the end of the night.

Nancy eyed the bottle and waved them in. "The dog stays out."

"If the dog stays out, so does the brandy."

"Fine, but if he soils the carpet, I'm sending you the bill."

"Agreed."

Nancy Guilford seemed to thrive on chaos and disarray. Items of high-quality clothing were draped over each chair, and lacy lingerie hung seductively from open drawers. Though the bed was made, thanks to the chambermaid, the quilt was untidy and shimmied out of place by recent use. There wasn't a book in sight, but a stack of movie magazines littered the table.

As she had with Mrs. Walsh, Haley claimed three glasses from their position beside the matching crystal decanter and set them on the sideboard in front of the candleholders. Ginger hovered over an open drawer, taking a moment to register the items—unfolded gloves topped by a crinkled receipt from a jewellery store—before closing it with her hip. She poured the brandy and passed a glass two fingers full to Nancy Guilford, who accepted with a nod of thanks.

"I suppose you figured out that the captain and I were lovers," she said after her first sip.

"We gathered that much." Ginger didn't think it necessary to say that they got the confirmation from the captain's wife.

"And you suspect me of being involved with his death."

"Were you?" Haley said.

Nancy took a big swig. "Nope."

Short and to the point. "Were you with him last night?" Ginger asked.

"Not that it's any of your business. But, yes." She

retrieved a cigarette from its case, inserted it into an ivory holder, and lit it with a silver lighter. Blowing smoke from the side of her mouth, she added, "And before you ask, he was alive when I left his room."

"Can you substantiate it?" Haley said.

Nancy Guilford glared back. "I don't have to provide an alibi to *you*."

"How well are you acquainted with Chief Officer MacIntosh?" Ginger said.

"This ain't none of your business, honey."

Ginger tried the same trick she had with Mrs. Walsh and presented the conversation as an opportunity to practice her answers to the police.

"How well are you acquainted with the chief officer?" Ginger repeated.

Nancy considered her before answering. "As well as anyone on this boat."

"Did you know that Captain Walsh was being blackmailed?"

Nancy scoffed. "Who told you that? Elise? She's delusional. She hated how Joseph preferred my company to hers and will do anything to cast a shadow over his memory."

"So, as far as you know, the captain wasn't being blackmailed."

"No, he was not." She stubbed out her half-smoked cigarette. "Now, if you don't mind, I'm feeling very tired and would like you to go."

Ginger examined the brandy bottle, with still a good third left, and sealed the top.

"Always a pleasure," Ginger said. Haley scoffed.

"Let's go, boy," Ginger urged Boss as she opened the door. She stopped short, having found herself nose to nose with Chief Inspector Reed, who had his fist up to knock.

"Chief Inspector Reed, what a surprise to see you here!"

His face tightened with a look of disgruntlement, an expression Ginger was beginning to believe was reserved for her. He eyed Boss with distaste, then said, "Is it? May I ask why *you* are here?"

Ginger waved the near-empty brandy bottle. "Just having a little tête-à-tête with our good friend, Nancy. Were you aware that she's a famous movie star? In America, that is."

"I'm afraid I haven't seen any of her films. Now, if you wouldn't mind," Chief Inspector Reed grumbled, "I would like to interview her."

"Most certainly, Chief Inspector," Ginger said with a victorious grin. "Good day."

CHAPTER TWELVE

With her broad-rimmed hat adorned with white silk flowers, and her delicate lacy gloves that nearly reached her elbows, Ginger believed she rivalled the actress when it came to glamour. She leaned back onto the lounge chair and daintily propped up one knee beneath the smoky blue crinkled silk of her Canton crepe frock. The breeze blew the oriental *crêpe-de-chine* trim of the skirt and bell sleeves in elegant waves. When a case required solving in a limited amount of time, taking a moment to enjoy the sun might seem frivolous, but Ginger needed a chance to pause and think. She closed her eyes. Every puzzle could be solved if studied from all angles.

Captain Walsh had been bludgeoned and transported to the cool pantry for preservation. The scene of the crime was unknown, at least to her. Those in relationship to the captain were all possible suspects.

"Just the person I was looking for."

Ginger smiled at the familiar voice before opening her eyes. "Ah, Chief Inspector Reed. Have you come to enjoy the lovely view?"

"I wish I had opportunity for leisure, Mrs. Gold, but alas, I have a murderer to apprehend."

Ginger sat up and adjusted her sunhat, ensuring the blue and green floral adornment was situated properly over her ear. "A trite inconvenience to one's relaxation."

"Quite right." The chief inspector removed his Panama straw hat and indicated to the empty lounge chair. "May I join you?"

Attracted to his confident air and admiring the handsome face the good Lord had given him, Ginger stared at the man. She especially appreciated his sense of style, noting his crisp tweed suit with a good crease down the trousers and his two-tone brogue shoes. She smiled. "Of course."

Instead of relaxing into a vacant lounger with legs outstretched, Chief Inspector Reed balanced at the foot end and leaned his elbows on his knees.

"You look serious," Ginger said.

"I am. I've heard from Scotland Yard. Are you aware that Captain Walsh owed your father money?"

Ginger blinked. "No, I'm not. How much?"

"A good deal. Ten thousand American dollars."

"What?" Ginger's mouth dropped open. "I had no idea."

Basil Reed eyed her carefully before asking, "Are you sure about that?"

"Chief Inspector Reed, what are you suggesting?"

"Perhaps the captain refused to pay up."

Ginger scoffed. "So, I smacked him over the head a couple times, dragged him to the pantry, and stuffed him into the pickle barrel."

"Not on your own, perhaps. You would've needed help. From a friend?"

"Who? Do you mean Miss Higgins? Most certainly not!"

The chief inspector made a show of looking around the deck. Only a few of the lounge chairs were occupied. "Where is the good nurse?"

"Miss Higgins remains in the room, her nose in a book. She's quite serious about her studies."

"As a doctor in training, Miss Higgins likely knows how to stop a heart."

"I'm sure she could come up with something far more interesting than bludgeoning, which wasn't what killed the captain, by the way."

"For the moment, I only have Nurse Higgins's word on that."

Ginger huffed. *Men.*

A bank of clouds rolled in, marring the once-bright blue sky. The wind stirred forcefully, and Ginger's skirt billowed upwards, revealing a shapely calf. Ginger quickly adjusted the hem.

Basil Reed cleared his throat and set his gaze back to hers. "Mrs. Gold, did you bring a revolver onboard?"

"Chief Inspector!"

"A gun is just another fashion accessory for Americans, but we English take our weapons more seriously."

"I don't see how my having a revolver or not is relevant. The captain didn't die of a gunshot wound."

"Please answer the question."

"Oh, drat it. Yes. *Yes, I did.* A nice little muff pistol."

"Make and model?"

Ginger stilled, pushing down her annoyance. She jutted her chin out in defiance. "Remington derringer, model 95. Cute little thing." Daniel had given it to her before he left

Boston to join the British Army. "Are you going to take it from me?"

"Why do you carry it?"

"I'm a woman travelling alone to a foreign land."

"England is hardly foreign to you, and you have a travel companion."

"Also a woman. We are both vulnerable."

Basil Reed raised a brow but conceded. "I'll allow it for now, so long as you promise to register it in London when you get there."

"Why should I do that? I'm not planning to stay."

"Then keep it out of sight unless absolutely necessary. If you find your plans change, come to the station. I'll assess your situation and consider registering permission."

Ginger could hardly contain her indignation. Sensing his master's strong emotion, Boss slunk out from under Ginger's chair.

"Whoa," Chief Inspector Reed said, jerking back. "I thought dogs weren't allowed on deck."

"Boss prefers my company, and he's really no trouble at all, so long as I keep him out of sight."

Chief Inspector Reed gave her a sideways glance. "I perceive you are one who doesn't mind bending the rules. I have to ask, Mrs. Gold, do you always get your way?"

"No." Not always.

"But often?"

Ginger no longer cared that Chief Inspector Reed was handsome or charming. "What's your point?"

His lips tugged up to one side. "I'd say don't leave town, but as we're on the *Rosa*, you've nowhere to go." Boss let out a low growl of displeasure. Chief Inspector Reed took a careful step back. Was the good Chief Inspector afraid of dogs? Ginger stifled a smirk.

"Mrs. Gold, isn't a clandestine pet outing ambitious and a little daring?"

Ginger shrugged and batted her eyelids with innocence. "Those are words I like to live my life by—ambitious and daring. In fact, I want those very words written on my tombstone when I die."

Basil Reed's jaw slackened, but then he pressed his lips firmly together.

Boss emitted another low belly growl.

"Boss doesn't seem to like you, Chief Inspector Reed, which is odd," Ginger said curtly. "He's usually such a good judge of character."

CHAPTER THIRTEEN

"That man is infuriating!" Ginger tossed her hat onto her bed as Boss reclaimed his spot on the pillow.

Haley sat up with interest. "Which man?"

Ginger peeled off her gloves with exaggerated flair. "Chief Chief Inspector Basil Reed."

"Full name declaration. Must be love."

"This is no time for jokes, Haley. He suspects me—us, actually—of murder."

Haley looked stunned. "That's ridiculous."

Ginger bobbed her head. "It most certainly is! Apparently, Captain Walsh owed my father money. Even if I had known about that, which I hadn't—you know how tight-lipped Father was when it came to finances—why would I kill him? I certainly wouldn't be any richer."

"Well," Haley said, tapping her lips with a pencil. "Assuming you were behaving logically and not full of passion and spite."

"I'm not spiteful! The chief inspector is still in one piece."

"For now."

Ginger calmed enough to sit on the mattress and unbuckle her suede double-strapped shoes. "I may be passionate, but I'm not vengeful."

"Perhaps I am, then," Haley said with a smirk. "Perhaps I knew about the injustice and killed the captain in a failed attempt to honour your father's memory."

"Haley Higgins! You mustn't joke like that!"

Haley chuckled. "I couldn't have moved him to the pantry without help, and you're the only friend I have."

Ginger was warmed by Haley's admission. In normal circumstances, they wouldn't have forged a friendship, each of them running in different circles—Ginger part of the upper class and Haley in the middle. If it weren't for her ailing father, and the wartime experiences they shared—a nightmare that removed social class and equalised men—they'd never have met.

"As much as the chief inspector's suspicions offend me, I suppose he is merely doing his job," Ginger said. "I can't begrudge him that."

"There's common sense talking."

Ginger poked at the air. "We must get into the captain's room."

"And there goes the common sense."

"I'm serious, Haley, and you need to be too. We must clear our names."

"And trespassing in a dead man's room will help us to do that how?"

"We won't know until we do it, now, will we?"

With Boss walking inconspicuously between them, they headed for the Walshes' staterooms.

Haley glanced at the dog. "Do you think it is a good idea to bring Boss?"

"Boss is very bright. He might sniff out something we'd miss."

"Or bark and give us away."

"He won't bark if I tell him not to."

"Smartest canine on the planet."

"You said it, and Boss and I both heard it." The terrier's knob of a tail shimmied in response.

They stopped at Mrs. Walsh's door, and Ginger knocked.

"Mrs. Walsh?"

There was every chance Mrs. Walsh would be in her room, but even as a newly minted widow, she wouldn't be expected to ride out the rest of the journey trapped in her personal quarters. Ginger tapped on the door and called out again, but it remained quiet on the other side. Haley tried the knob. "It's locked."

Ginger removed a hairpin from her hat, wiggled it through the keyhole, and moments later the lock gave.

"Mrs. Gold, you never fail to amaze me."

"The war," Ginger said in way of explanation. She'd learned a great many unorthodox skills while serving in France. "Come, Boss."

The room looked much the same as it had that morning. Ginger took the opportunity to sneak a search of the drawers. Plain Victorian underthings—bloomers, stockings, corsets—no face powders or jewellery, just a few hat pins. Mrs. Walsh was a no-nonsense woman.

Haley took a peek in the wardrobe. "Anything?" Ginger asked.

"Nothing out of the ordinary," Haley said. "Several well-made dresses in dark shades of blue, grey, and black." She gave Ginger a look. "Well-stocked widow fare, if she was preparing for such a thing, and a variety of black tie-up boots. Mrs. Walsh might not have your fashion sense, but she has a good tailor."

"Do you think her wardrobe indicates premeditation?"

"That or her sense of style is legitimately worse than mine."

At the back of the stocking drawer, Ginger discovered a shiny silver square.

"Well, look at this," she said. With gloved hands, she held up a cuff link engraved with a fleur-de-lis.

"The captain's cuff links?" Haley said.

Ginger ran her fingers along the bottom and edges of the drawer. "Cuff link. There's only one."

"It's not so unusual for a wife to be in possession of her husband's belongings," Haley said.

As Ginger had hoped, the door between the two rooms was unlocked, which surprised her, considering Miss Guilford admitted to being a frequent visitor. Surely the captain had had enough respect for his wife that he would've at least locked the door.

Then again maybe he *had* locked the door and it was the wife who had unlocked it and entered.

The room was an inverse duplicate of Elise Walsh's. A quick search through the drawers and wardrobe produced a male version of the same sort of belongings.

"Surely we're not the first to poke around," Haley said.

Ginger agreed. "The good Chief Inspector must be doing something to earn his reputation. Certainly this was the first place he came."

Ginger found a fine mahogany box filled with a nice assortment of cuff links. "No solos in here," she said.

Boss sniffed the carpet in an area behind a chair next to the window and whined.

"What is it, Bossy?" Ginger followed him to a barely

noticeable dark splatter that marred the pattern of the red carpet.

"Looks like something bad happened here," Ginger said.

Haley joined them and squatted to take a closer look. "Blood."

Ginger pointed to the sideboard. "One of the candleholders is missing."

"I thought they were secured?"

Ginger leaned over and squinted. "It appears they can be unfastened. Probably so the maids can clean them."

Haley straightened and brushed out her skirt. "I'd wager a bet that the missing candleholder is the murder weapon."

"So, this is the scene of the crime," Ginger mused. "But how did the killer get the body to the cold pantry three decks below? Even a strong man would get winded with dead weight over his back like a sack of potatoes."

"A laundry cart perhaps, or a service trolley?"

"Ah, good thinking, Haley. The captain would quite likely arrange for something to be brought up if he planned to entertain."

"We have to consider that it's possible we're dealing with more than one killer," Haley said. "Two working together for a common goal."

"Or maybe *not* a common goal," Ginger said. "Perhaps there are two motives and the killers discovered that they each wanted the captain dead for different reasons and colluded."

"Good hypothesis," Haley said. "Let's say you're right. Who would our couple team players be?"

"Nancy Guilford and MacIntosh? Elise Walsh and Babineaux?"

The sound of voices travelled from Mrs. Walsh's room. Ginger stared at Boss and held a finger to her lips. She was going to have to give him an extra treat when they got back to their room.

The door adjoining the rooms was left open a crack, enough for Ginger and Haley to witness Mrs. Walsh alone with Babineaux.

"I may have despised him," Elise said, "but that doesn't mean I wanted him dead."

"*Le monde verra cela comme tragique, mais pour nous, chère Elise, cela signifie la liberté.*"

Ginger gave Haley a raised brow and whispered, "The world will see this as tragic, but for us, dear Elise, it means freedom."

CHAPTER FOURTEEN

Ginger and Haley eased out of the main door from the captain's room and into the corridor.

Keeping her voice low, Haley asked, "Was that an admission of guilt by Babineaux?"

"It certainly could be interpreted as such," Ginger said. "However, he didn't actually say he did it."

"Your suspicions about Babineaux and Mrs. Walsh were spot-on," Haley said. "His affection for her could be considered motive."

Ginger nodded. "I agree."

"So, what now?"

"I'm not sure. I'll take Boss for a little walk and think on it."

"I'll meet you back in the room later." Haley turned in the direction of the port side and Ginger continued on.

On deck, many of the passengers took advantage of the sunshine. Mr. and Mrs. Fairchild waved when they spotted Ginger. She waved in return but picked up her pace, pointing to the dog to indicate she was in a hurry to take him below—a ruse to prevent a lengthy social entanglement.

After more than one frown and a mutter of disapproval at Boss's presence, Ginger lifted him into her arms, allowing the *crêpe-de-chine* of her bell sleeves to conceal him. An upswing of wind caught hold of the rim of her hat, and if it hadn't been for her excellent reflexes, she might have lost it. She pressed it firmly in place with one hand.

She was debating her next move when fate intervened. Patty Applebalm hurried by, a white-gloved hand also trapping her hat on her head.

Ginger turned on her heel and followed.

"Miss Applebalm!"

The lady shot a startled look over her shoulder.

"Hello!" Ginger said with a friendly smile. "I don't think we've been officially introduced. I'm Mrs. Gold."

Patty Applebalm hesitated before answering. "How do you do?"

"Just fine, thank you. You?"

"Very well."

Ginger stepped into stride beside the lady, who wore a day dress in a shade of peach that did not flatter her skin colour. Ginger was surprised that Miss Guilford hadn't pointed it out. Or maybe she had, and Miss Applebalm ignored her advice. Though the assistant had a mousy, unassuming air about her, one couldn't work for someone like Nancy Guilford if one didn't have at least a little spunk.

"Have you worked for Miss Guilford long?" Ginger asked. "It must be such an exciting job, assisting a famous film star."

Patty Applebalm considered Ginger as if she wasn't quite sure about the level of intelligence she was dealing with. "I've known Miss Guilford all her life."

Ginger noted that Patty didn't actually answer either question.

"Are you her aunt?"

Patty glanced at her sharply. "Why do you ask that?"

"Well, you said you've known her all her life, and I do see a slight resemblance." It was a *very* slight resemblance, as in hardly at all, but Ginger hoped her exaggeration would draw the woman out. She was rewarded.

"It's not widely known, but Nancy is my twin sister's child. Sadly, my sister is no longer with us."

"I'm sorry. It's fortunate that Miss Guilford still has you at her side."

"I love her as my own. It's very gracious for Nancy to employ me. There are hundreds of young girls who'd be happy to take my job, and more qualified too."

"A mutually beneficial arrangement, then."

"Well, yes."

Boss wiggled in Ginger's arm, and Patty Applebalm's hand flew to her chest. "Good golly! I didn't notice your dog."

"Oh, please do excuse him. He didn't mean to frighten you. He's really such a gentleman."

"He is a . . . funny-looking sort of thing."

Ginger blinked but retained her smile, ignoring the insult to her beloved pet. "He's a Boston terrier, a terrier and boxer mix. The breed is all the rage in America."

Patty harrumphed.

"You're not a dog person, I take it?"

"I prefer cats," Patty said. "I had to leave Peanut and Butter at home. It's not so easy to transport cats."

"I'm sure they miss you."

Ginger caught sight of the rising waves, and her stomach turned as the ship lilted. She dreaded the thought of being tossed about at sea. Once in a lifetime was enough.

"I really must hurry back," Patty Applebalm said. "Miss Guilford is expecting me."

"Of course. Please give my regards to Miss Guilford."

Ginger and Miss Applebalm parted ways, leaving Ginger alone. It was then that she heard someone hissing.

"*Psst!*"

Ginger stilled and turned to the sound.

"*Psst*, miss."

Ginger scanned the deck for young Scout, knowing the lad would be in deep water if he was caught in first class. She had to give him credit—though she heard him, she couldn't see him anywhere. He was as invisible as he'd claimed.

She could've had Boss sniff him out, but she didn't want to draw attention.

"Meet me by the engine room," she said aloud to seemingly no one, catching the odd look from a grey-haired couple strolling past.

Ginger meandered languidly, keeping an impassive expression on her face, but inside she raged with curiosity. Young Scout must have something important to tell her if he felt it merited the huge risk he took to find her.

Scout sat on a bench across from a stack of wooden, whitewashed lifeboats. He was so small—much smaller than a boy his age should be—that his bare feet dangled in the air. Ginger's heart pinged. Her dog's life was better than this young boy's. The unsatisfied maternal piece of her soul longed to sweep him up and take him home. Give him a warm bath and a hot bowl of soup. A haircut and a toothbrush. A teddy bear and a hug. But she knew there were hundreds more just like Scout in London, and she'd left as many behind in Boston. At least she could help this one by giving him these little jobs.

"Scout," she said as she approached.

He stretched out to pet Boss. "'Ello, ol' boy." Then to Ginger, "'Ello, miss."

"Why don't you call me Mrs. Gold," she said. "We're friends now, aren't we?"

"Yes, miss—I mean, missus!"

Ginger smiled. Scout's enthusiasm was contagious. "What do you have for me, young man?"

She expected him to produce the missing silver cuff link, for which she was prepared to compensate him with a generous tip.

Scout stood and twitched with restrained excitement. "Ya told me ter tell ya if I saw summit 'spicious, right?"

"Yes."

"*Oi*, I seen summit real 'spicious-like."

"What did you see?"

"I saw a lady throw summit over the rails."

"Did you see what it was?"

Scout frowned. "No, but it were about this long." He held out his small hands to the length of a loaf of bread. "And heavy-like. She throw'd it over and . . . and it made a good splash."

"Where did this happen?"

"Right over there, missus. Be'ind the engine room."

"Did you recognise the woman?"

"Nah. She had 'er back to me and a big ol' 'at on 'er 'ead. The sun were in me eyes."

His grubby hand extended forward, holding a palm-sized square sheet of paper. "She dropped this."

It was a photograph of a toddler dressed in trousers and a simple white shirt. Ginger flipped it over, and the handwriting on the back was simply a child's name. Joseph Jr.

CHAPTER FIFTEEN

From the corner of her eye, Ginger detected Chief Inspector Reed heading up the steps to first class.

"Scout, would you mind Boss for me for a little while? I'll pick him up in the kennel later on."

"Sure thing, missus."

Ginger handed over Boss' leash, reassured him that she'd come for him soon, and sprinted up to first class. She didn't see the chief inspector right away and worried that she'd lost him, but then caught sight of him on the metal steps that led to the bridge. His suit jacket flapped in the wind, and he held his felt hat to his head.

Hand on her own summer hat, Ginger followed the chief inspector. She was careful to keep a good distance in case he should glance over his shoulder. From this vantage point, she could see passengers meandering about on both the first- and second-class decks. The sun shone brightly as it set in the west, while contrasting dark, brooding clouds rolled in from the east. The waves, once calm, were as choppy as meringue. The air smelled metallic with the promise of a change in the weather. Ginger only hoped they'd reach Liverpool before a storm broke.

Ginger called out to Chief Inspector Reed just as he positioned his fist to knock on the door to the bridge. "Chief Inspector!"

He turned to her in surprise. "Mrs. Gold? Can I help you?"

Ginger smiled brightly. "I'm assuming you're about to interview Chief Officer MacIntosh. Would you permit me to join you?"

A deep V formed between his hazel eyes. "Surely, you must be aware that civilians aren't typically invited to get involved in an open murder investigation." His frown deepened. "Especially those who find themselves a suspect."

Ginger ignored the last part of his statement. "Well, yes, I'm sure it's not typical in a city like London. However, with only you onboard to investigate and only one day left before we reach Liverpool, I would think that you would appreciate a little assistance."

The chief inspector folded his arms, the crisp linen of his suit crinkling at the elbows. "And how is it that you can assist me?"

"I have some information you might find helpful."

Basil Reed raised a brow. "Go on."

"If I give you what I know, I think it only fair that you allow me to accompany you." She held up a palm. "Before you say anything, consider this—entering with a female companion would put the officer at ease. He won't suspect that you are interviewing him as a potential murder suspect, and therefore would likely be more forthcoming."

"You drive a hard bargain," The chief inspector said, relenting. "Very well, you may join me, so long as you promise to let me do all the talking."

Ginger pantomimed turning a key in front of her mouth.

"So, what is this piece of news that you have?" The chief inspector said.

"Miss Higgins and I were walking Boss, and we happened to witness Officer MacIntosh leaving Miss Guilford's private room." She stared at him with meaning. "Quite alone."

"I see."

"In fact, the incident occurred shortly before you arrived to interview her."

"You seem to spend a lot of time on the starboard side of the ship. It is my understanding that your room is situated on the port side."

Ginger batted her eyes. "How is it, Chief Inspector, that you would know exactly where my own private room is?"

"As the investigating officer of this crime, it is my duty to know where every passenger is situated and located."

Ginger found that broad-stroke explanation disappointing. She enjoyed being the centre of attention and wouldn't have minded if the chief inspector had specifically sought her out.

"Fair enough," she said. "Shall we go in?"

Chief Inspector Reed knocked on the door, and it was answered by a sailor who announced their arrival to Chief Officer MacIntosh, now the acting captain.

MacIntosh didn't seem surprised to see the chief inspector though he did raise a brow at the presence of Ginger Gold.

"And to what do I owe this honour?"

"If you would permit me," Chief Inspector Reed said, "I have a few questions."

MacIntosh considered Ginger with appraising eyes.

Knowing that he was a ladies' man, Ginger winked to give him the false impression that perhaps she would be interested, should Miss Guilford become unavailable. MacIntosh sat casually in the captain's chair just as Ginger predicted.

"Officer MacIntosh," Chief Inspector Reed began. "How has the demise of Captain Walsh affected you and the goings-on here on the bridge?"

"Of course, we are all saddened and shocked by his death," MacIntosh replied solemnly. "But as the next-in-line senior officer, it is now my obligation and duty to ensure that the passengers of the SS *Rosa* get to Liverpool safely."

Basil Reed scribbled in a small notepad. "If I understand correctly, as second-in-command, you are now the acting captain of this ship."

"That's true."

The chief inspector looked the chief officer in the eye. "Will that be a permanent position?"

MacIntosh didn't break his gaze. "The final decision is not mine, though it is common for the first officer to replace the captain if he's suddenly indisposed, and so long as there's no other officer with more seniority who wants this post."

"And is there anybody else that you know of who would want this post?"

MacIntosh stiffened. "I wouldn't know that, sir."

"Did you and the captain get on?"

"If you mean did we drink beer together in our free time, no, but onboard, we were both professionals."

"What were you and the captain quarrelling about on the bridge?" Ginger asked, earning a scowl from the chief inspector.

"I don't know what you mean?"

"I saw you, you know I did."

"Oh, that? Just a silly disagreement."

"Over what, precisely?" Chief Inspector Reed asked with interest.

MacIntosh let out a short breath. "Walsh owed me money and refused to pay. He didn't take it kindly when I threatened to go public."

That lined up with Elise Walsh's blackmailing story, Ginger thought. The captain was struggling to pay up.

"What exactly is your relationship with Miss Nancy Guilford?" she asked.

Chief Inspector Reed shot her a warning glance, but nodded to MacIntosh. "Answer the question."

"There is no relationship between myself and Miss Guilford," MacIntosh said. "She's a passenger on the *Rosa*, and I, as a senior crew member of the ship, go out of my way to spend time with all the passengers. We want happy and satisfied customers."

"Miss Guilford looked very *happy and satisfied* to me," Ginger said. "Oops." Her hand flew to her lips as she confronted Basil Reed's displeasure with a faux look of apology.

MacIntosh stood and tugged on his white blazer. "What exactly do you mean by that, Mrs. Gold?"

Chief Inspector Reed tapped Ginger's arm before she could answer, guiding her towards the door. "Thank you for your time, Officer MacIntosh," he said stiffly. "I'll find you if I have any further questions."

Back on deck, Basil Reed pierced Ginger with an intense glare. "I thought you said you were going to let me do all the talking."

"Did you see his face?" Ginger said. "He was rattled by

my question. He knows he was caught in a lie, and he tried to cover it up."

Chief Inspector Reed harrumphed, his frustration with Ginger ebbing. "He did seem quite shaken at your question, or rather, your outrageous accusation."

"Perhaps the actress and MacIntosh worked together," Ginger said.

"Why would you suggest that?'

"Well, MacIntosh and Captain Walsh were at odds over something. Maybe it wasn't money, but rather power. Perhaps MacIntosh was tired of playing second fiddle and didn't want to wait for the captain to retire."

"It's an interesting hypothesis."

"Or perhaps the motive has to do with... the alluring complexities of women."

"Do you think MacIntosh and Miss Guilford were, um, involved?"

Ginger arched a brow. "Miss Guilford is quite captivating, is she not?"

The chief inspector swallowed. "I hadn't noticed. However, if they colluded together, what would you say was Miss Guilford's motive?"

"She was tired of sharing the captain with his wife," Ginger said. "It's the classic mistress/wife tension. The man promises the girlfriend he'll leave the wife, but year after year goes by, and he never does."

"Why not just break it off with the captain? Killing him seems somewhat extreme."

Ginger propped a hand on her waist. "Have you never heard of a woman scorned?"

Basil Reed frowned. "I'm the first to admit that the complexities of the female population are a mystery."

CHAPTER SIXTEEN

Ginger couldn't keep from repeatedly glancing at the chief inspector who sat by himself on the other side of the breakfast room.

"Just admit it," Haley said with a grin. "You find him intriguing."

"I'll admit to no such thing!" Ginger sipped her coffee and deflected. "I wasn't looking at *him*. I merely caught sight of my new friend, Roy Hardy."

Haley glanced over her shoulder to confirm that the redheaded waiter was indeed working in the area where Chief Inspector Reed was busy reading a newspaper.

Ginger cast Haley a defiant look, then added, "I promised him I'd help him out with his heart's desire, but this murder case has preoccupied my thoughts and I haven't come up with a single idea."

Haley held out both of her palms, alternately raising and lowering them like a scale. "Murder, romance. Both not your business, I might add."

"*Pfft.*" Ginger's eyes betrayed her and sought out the chief inspector. He happened to glance up at the exact moment, and their gaze locked for a split second before she quickly looked away. She felt appalled. She was caught staring. What was the matter with her? Her skills since the war had slipped in dramatic measures! That was what five years of leisure would do, she supposed.

"What do you make of that baby photo?" Haley said. *She*, at least, could keep her mind steady on the case.

"I can't be certain it belonged to the woman Scout witnessed throwing the heavy item overboard," Ginger said with a sigh. "It could be merely coincidental that the child's name matched the captain's."

"Joseph is a common name." Haley held her near-empty coffee cup high and took the final sip. "And as far as we know, none of our suspects are parents."

"Perhaps it's a photo of a nephew."

"Or was dropped accidentally by someone else entirely and your little friend was mistaken about it coming from the mystery woman."

"Exactly. It might be a distraction rather than a clue."

Haley rose. "I'll leave you to your meddling, Mrs. Gold. Do find me if you discover anything juicy. And please, refrain from getting yourself killed."

"I'll do my best."

Ginger adjusted her cloche—a felt bell-shaped hat with virtually no rim—and donned her gloves. She wasn't quite ready to go, and she waved Roy Hardy over.

"More coffee, please."

"Yes, madam."

The waiter returned in short order and refilled Ginger's cup. She took the opportunity to engage him, whispering conspiratorially. "I've hired a lad from steerage to walk my dog, Boss. He's been instructed to meet Miss Chloe in front of my room at ten thirty—the boy has a pocket watch and is uncommonly timely. Go to number 45 under the pretence of delivering a bottle of wine at my request. However, I'll not be there, so give the bottle to Miss Chloe to place in my room."

Roy Hardy smiled. "Yes, madam."

"There is something imperative that you must do when you get there."

The waiter's expression grew serious. "Anything."

"You must introduce yourself to Miss Chloe."

Roy Hardy's face blanched and then reddened. "Madam? I don't..."

"Those are my terms. You've already engaged in conversation. Simply add these words, 'We've not been formally introduced. I'm Roy Hardy.' Can you do that?"

The waiter threw his shoulders back in determination. "Yes, madam."

"Good. Make it a fine French cabernet sauvignon, will you?"

Ginger's focus returned to the chief inspector, and this time she didn't glance away when he caught her looking. He folded his paper, tucked it under his arm, placed his bowler hat on his head, and walked towards her.

"Good morning, Mrs. Gold," he said when he reached her.

She smiled up at him. "Good morning, Chief Inspector."

He pointed to Haley's vacated chair. "May I?"

"Of course."

"Sleep well?" he asked politely.

"I did. You?"

"Like a log. I think it's the fresh sea air."

"The case doesn't keep you awake? I confess to finding it difficult to shut off my mind."

"Not at all. Rather, a good night's rest often is the key to solving a case. It's amazing what puzzles unlock the next morning over a good cup of coffee."

Ginger raised her cup. "And the coffee here is quite good."

"I agree."

She cocked her head coyly. "So, did you unlock the case?"

"Since you're so keen, perhaps I should ask you the same question?"

"I've been thinking about Miss Guilford. What if her motive isn't love or spite, but money? Perhaps the captain left something to her in his will? Maybe he broke things off with her, and she wanted to make sure that he didn't change the will when he returned to London."

Chief Inspector Reed inclined his head. "You are full of ideas, Mrs. Gold."

"I do read a lot of detective novels."

Her admission didn't get a nod of approval from the chief inspector.

"Yes, well, I see you've put some thought into this."

"It's obviously either Miss Guilford and Officer MacIntosh, or Mrs. Walsh and Babineaux."

"You are rather sure of yourself," Basil Reed said.

"I could be wrong on the matchup," Ginger added, "but I'm confident it's a team."

"One strong man could've carried this crime out on his own."

"Even a strong man would have had trouble lugging a dead body from the captain's bedroom down several decks to the ship's pantry."

Chief Inspector Reed paused for a beat as he studied

her. "How do you know the captain was killed in his bedroom?"

"Oh," Ginger said calmly, as if her trespass was of no consequence. "Miss Higgins and I visited with Mrs. Walsh to extend our condolences and to offer our assistance. Mrs. Walsh mentioned the captain's adjoining stateroom. When Mrs. Walsh was indisposed"—Ginger made it sound like Mrs. Walsh had just stepped out to powder her nose—"Miss Higgins and I took a peek in the captain's room. We saw a bloodstain on the carpet."

Chief Inspector Reed leaned back and uttered a sigh. "I'm not sure if I should be impressed or distressed by your interference into this investigation."

"Impressed, absolutely! And rest assured we never touched anything. We left everything as it was. We understand how modern forensics work. Were you able to collect fingerprints?"

"As a matter of fact, yes. However, since I lack an investigative team, I had to dust for prints myself. Unfortunately, I won't get data on them until after I return to the Yard."

"Have you identified the murder weapon?"

The chief inspector cleared this throat. "As of yet, it hasn't been located."

"I have a witness who observed a woman throw a heavy item overboard. It was about the size of a candleholder."

"You have a *witness*? Do tell!"

"Chief Inspector, I can't give my confidential informers away."

Basil Reed grunted in exasperation. "What makes you think the murder weapon was a candleholder?"

"One was missing in the captain's room. Surely you noticed that?"

"I did. I just didn't expect you to."

Ginger glared at him. "I'm not a silly, empty-minded woman, Basil Reed. I have a degree!"

Chief Inspector Reed's jaw slackened. "My apologies," he said. He had the decency to look sufficiently contrite. "I didn't mean to offend. Young girls these days seem unable to take anything seriously, it's just all parties and fun. I shouldn't have judged you."

Ginger allowed for a small smile. "Apology accepted. But I'll have you know I'm not that young. I'm twenty-nine." Actually, she had turned thirty the month previous, but she couldn't quite make herself admit to it.

The chief inspector who was a good decade her senior, only nodded. "So, did your witness identify the woman?"

"Alas, her back was to him and she wore a large hat. And the sun was in his eyes."

"Convenient."

"I trust him implicitly."

Basil Reed crossed his legs and held a finger to his chin. "Just because a woman throws an item overboard, doesn't mean it's linked to this case."

"I agree," Ginger said. "Only, the murder weapon is still missing, so until it's found, we can't dismiss it."

"Fine. It only means a woman could be involved, which we've already concluded was a possibility."

"It points to the woman being responsible for bludgeoning the captain. Her accomplice may just have been recruited to help dispose of the body."

"Which takes us back to your theory of a perpetrator team."

"Yes."

"Okay, *Chief Inspector* Gold," Basil Reed said with a sly grin. "What would you do next?"

Ginger smiled brightly. "I'd interview the cook."

CHAPTER SEVENTEEN

The kitchen was busy, and Babineaux straightened in surprise at the sight of Ginger and the chief inspector walking into what he considered to be his personal domain. He collected himself and tossed a towel into one of the big stainless-steel sinks. "Chief Inspector, *Meesus* Gold, how can I help?"

"I can see how busy you are. Sorry to disturb you," Chief Inspector Reed said. "I would like to ask you a few questions if you could spare a few minutes."

"Of course. My office *eez* private and more comfortable." Babineaux spoke to his kitchen crew in French, giving them instructions and telling them he'd be away momentarily. Then, in English, he asked Ginger and the chief inspector, "Can I offer you coffee or a tea?"

Both Ginger and the chief inspector declined. Babineaux poured himself a cup of coffee, drinking it black.

The chief inspector took a seat at the desk opposite Babineaux. Ginger claimed the empty chair next to the chief inspector.

"I can assume the reasons as to why you are here, Chief

Inspector," Babineaux said. "But if I may, why in the company of Mrs. Gold?"

Even though the question was directed at the chief inspector, Ginger took the liberty of answering. "To observe as a witness, should there be a need for this conversation to come up in court." Her response surprised both the cook and the chief inspector, but neither said anything to refute her.

"You discovered the body"—Basil Reed made a point of staring into his notebook—"at 8:00 a.m. yesterday morning."

"Yes, sir. I was thinking about the menu and *eet* occurred to me that maybe the strawberries were *fini*."

"I see," Basil Reed said. "What attracted you to the pickle barrel?"

"I have already told you all of this, Chief Inspector," Babineaux said, looking uncomfortable.

"Please humour me. A lot was going on at that time, and I want to make sure that I jotted down my facts straight."

Babineaux's shoulders seemed to relax a little. "I was about to retrieve the last pickles in the barrel, when I noticed a sticky patch on the floor. The kitchen and pantry are always kept in *teep*-top order. I was about to gather a mop when I saw the lid on the barrel was ajar."

"Tell us about your relationship with Mrs. Walsh," Ginger asked.

Babineaux jerked, spilling his coffee. Chief Inspector Reed pursed his lips as if he was holding in his annoyance, then nodded to the cook, indicating he'd like an answer.

Babineaux mopped up his spill with the hem of his apron. "Mrs. Walsh and I are acquainted because she *eez* the wife of the captain. She frequently travels with her husband to America. All of the kitchen staff know her. In fact, she enjoys cooking and likes to lend a hand on occasion."

"And Captain Walsh was all right with this arrangement?"

The cook grunted. "To be quite honest, Captain Walsh was not the most attentive husband. At least not until this trip."

"Why do you say that?"

"It was the first time the captain noticed his wife *een* the kitchen. He shouted at her and ordered her out. He said the wife of a ship's captain should not associate with the likes of us." Babineaux could no longer hide the disdain in his voice.

"You didn't like the captain, did you?" The chief inspector said.

"Matters not if I liked the man or not. I *deed* my job."

"It does where the captain's wife is concerned," Chief Inspector Reed said.

The cook flushed red and began to babble. "*Meesus* Walsh deserved better than *heem* . . . Captain Walsh was good at his job, but as a husband—*merde*." His gaze cut to Ginger. "Excuse my French, madame."

"And if the captain was to suddenly disappear?" Chief Inspector Reed said. "Surely it would free your 'friend' from what you view as mistreatment."

"I *do* view it as mistreatment!"

Haley would like this guy, Ginger thought.

Babineaux blundered on. "I *deed not keel* the captain if that *ees* what you are implying."

"Not even for love?" Ginger said. Her question caught the cook off guard. He was mid-sip of his coffee, and he spat it out, hitting the chief inspector in the face. Ginger blinked in disgust as spittle landed on her dress.

"*Excusez-moi!*" Babineaux called for help from the

kitchen, and a sailor scurried over with a towel. He awkwardly attempted to pat the coffee off the chief inspector. Basil Reed snatched the towel from the sailor's hand and dabbed at the coffee on his suit and his face. He gave the cloth to Ginger. She pouted, wondering if her Canton crepe was now ruined.

"*Eet* just went down the wrong way," Babineaux explained. "I do apologise."

"It's quite all right, ol' chap," The chief inspector said, standing. "If I have any more questions, I will find you."

Out of earshot of the kitchen staff, Ginger leaned in to the chief inspector and said, "That was very suspicious, wouldn't you say?"

CHAPTER EIGHTEEN

Ginger's pulse leapt at the thought of the upcoming ballroom dance. She loved dancing almost as much as she loved fashion. She flipped through her gowns and placed them on her bed one by one.

Haley's head bobbed up from her books. "What are you doing?"

"I can never decide exactly what to wear," Ginger said.

"Can't you examine your wardrobe without undoing all the work we went through to hang them up?"

Ginger's attention moved from the dresses to Haley's face. Her friend hadn't sounded angry or frustrated, and Ginger was satisfied that she was merely interested in Ginger's modus operandi.

"I need to see them in the light," Ginger said. She rested a long, painted fingernail on her chin. "I'm waiting for one to call out to me."

"Now I'm worried."

Ginger shot Haley a look. "I'm not going crazy. At least not yet."

"Noted."

"It's just that these dresses are all so gorgeous: I almost feel like I would be cheating one by selecting the other. You must help me decide."

Haley cast her a look of helplessness. "You've a very nice selection of gowns, but—and don't take this the wrong way—outside of colour, they all look the same to me."

"Haley Higgins! That's heresy!"

Haley snorted.

Ginger tried on a blue loose-fitting dress with a long, full skirt and a large, full-bloom starched rose fastened at the hip. She examined her reflection in the mirror, frowned, and discarded it.

"What was wrong with that one?"

"I don't know. It just didn't feel right."

After two more attempts, Ginger felt she'd hit a home run with a gold, straight-lined chemise dress with two shimmering layers that flowed from the waist. It was tastefully decorated with tiny metal sequins, sleeveless, with a wide bateau neckline that accentuated the creamy contours around Ginger's collarbones. She chose a very fashionable, beaded turban-like headdress and finished her look off with super-sheer hose and black strappy two-inch heels.

"How about this?"

"It's great. You look beautiful."

"That's what you said about the others."

Haley shrugged, but didn't deny the charge.

Ginger looked at her friend dejectedly. "Oh, I miss Molly."

Haley said grumpily, "I'm beginning to miss her too."

Ginger, ignoring Haley's veiled complaint, appealed to her appreciation of history. "Did you know the ballroom on this vessel used to be the triage room during the war?"

"Is that so?" Haley replied.

"Yes. The lives of many men were saved there by nurses like you."

"Interesting."

"Shouldn't you like to come to see it?"

"Nope."

"*Pfft*, Haley, you're impossible."

"I've been called worse."

"You're sure I can't convince you to come along? It seems a shame for you to miss such an elegant event."

"Dances are really of no interest to me," Haley said. "I'd rather stay in and read."

"All work and no play makes Jack a dull boy," Ginger said twirling on the tips of her shoes. "In this case. it makes Haley a dull girl."

"I'm sure you'll have enough fun for both of us." Haley leaned back and propped bare feet onto an empty chair. "I'm assuming that the dashing Chief Inspector will be there?"

"It's quite likely," Ginger said. "He is a fine dancer after all. But don't think for a minute that I'm going to spend my evening dancing with him. There are plenty of gentlemen onboard to keep me occupied until the early morning hours."

"I'm almost tempted to come just to watch you. You're a delightful spectacle on the dance floor."

"Does that mean you've changed your mind?" Ginger asked hopefully.

Haley smirked. "I'm afraid not."

* * *

One truly had to use their imagination to picture the ballroom as a bloody, noisy triage centre. All traces of death and dying had been painted over and polished. The wooden floor glistened under the lights of the chandeliers that hung from an ornate ceiling. Plush, upholstered chairs in rich greens and pinks sat in clusters along the walls. The bar in the back was made of rich mahogany, with brass rails to hold in flyaway glasses.

Ginger spotted Roy Hardy working at the bar and strolled over. He was dressed in a crisp, clean uniform, and his red hair was neatly combed over from a straight side parting.

"Mr. Hardy," she said in greeting.

"Good evening, Mrs. Gold," Roy Hardy returned with a friendly smile. "Might I get you something to drink?"

"Yes, please. A glass of your best champagne."

"Most certainly."

Ginger watched him as he skilfully popped the cork, poured several ounces into a tall flute, and handed it to her.

"How did it go with Miss Chloe?" she asked.

Roy Hardy's face flushed crimson. "I did as you said, madam."

"And?"

"It's hard to say. We're now formally introduced, but I'm no more certain as to whether I've turned her heart."

"Baby steps, Mr. Hardy."

"Madam, is there something I should do next?"

Ginger nodded. "You must do some investigating on your own as to when Miss Chloe takes her lunch break. Then arrange for yourself to have a break during that time. When you see her, ask if you can join her. If she says yes, you have your answer that she is interested. If she makes an excuse, or agrees, but without a smile, the answer is no."

Roy Hardy swallowed hard. "I think my stomach will not be able to handle a meal either way."

"Better to know where you stand upfront, no? If she's not interested, you won't waste your time any further.

There are plenty of other girls who would be happy to spend time with you."

Roy Hardy waited a beat before asking, "Do you think so?"

The young waiter had little in the way of self-confidence, and Ginger was determined to bolster it.

"Absolutely, Mr. Hardy. You're ambitious, intelligent, and handsome. You must see yourself as such and move forward boldly."

"Thank you, madam," Roy Hardy said, smiling ear to ear. "Thank you, so very much."

Ginger did as she had promised Haley and spent half the evening dancing with every available gentleman who was willing, but not Chief Chief Inspector Reed. It came to a point when he was among the few left who had not asked her to dance. Ginger was tempted to harbour offence at this slight. She found herself seeking him out in the room despite her current dancing partner, and chastised herself for this weakness, even though she found that the chief inspector was doing the same. It was quite ridiculous how they both pretended to ignore each other.

Eventually he crossed the room and asked for a dance. She held up a gloved hand and obliged.

"You've been quite busy on your feet tonight, Mrs. Gold. I hope you still have a morsel of energy left to spare for me?"

"I believe I do, Chief Inspector."

Ginger placed her hand on Basil Reed's shoulder as he gently placed one of his on her upper back. Their alternate hands joined, and Basil Reed expertly waltzed her across the ballroom floor.

"Have you gotten any further on the case, Chief Inspector Reed?" Ginger asked.

"You certainly get right to the point," he said. He hesitated as if he was wrestling with himself, whether he should share his findings with her, and in the end, he relented.

"I interviewed Miss Patty Applebalm, and she revealed to me that she is not only Miss Guilford's assistant, but is also related by blood. Miss Guilford is her sister's daughter."

"I had guessed as much." Ginger didn't feel it prudent to mention that she too had queried the woman.

"Had you?"

"Indeed. I perceived a familiarity between the two women that went beyond an employer and her employee. It was natural to assume that there was a kinship somewhere." On Basil Reed's look of doubt, she added, "Miss Higgins can confirm my suspicions."

He inhaled, accepting Ginger's explanation. "It seems that the Applebalm family were humble farmers in Eastern America. Apparently, Miss Guilford works hard to keep this fact out of the press." He cocked his head. "Did you perceive that as well?"

"I'm afraid not," Ginger said. "I am a good study of character, but I have yet to master mind reading."

"I'm relieved to hear that, Mrs. Gold. I was beginning to think that you were some kind of mystical creature and not flesh and blood."

Ginger broke into her sprightly laugh. "There is nothing to fear there, my dear Chief Inspector. I am as human as you are."

"Yet above average, I would say. I regret that I must confess to having made inquiries about you." As an afterthought, he added, "As I have with all my suspects."

Ginger pulled back and stared into Basil Reed's eyes. "Oh?"

"It seems that you have more skills than you let on. Skills that came in handy during the war."

Ginger kept her expression blank. "I have no idea what you mean."

"It seems that even Scotland Yard can't access the total of your files. Your activities were quite confidential."

Ginger smiled playfully. "I feel you have me mistaken for someone else. My task during the war was simple. I operated the telephone switchboard in France, nothing more."

Basil Reed didn't respond. They swirled around the floor in silence until the song ended. Ginger couldn't be sure just how much the chief inspector knew about her covert activities during the war, but that was no longer her concern. She kept her side of the bargain by remaining silent.

CHAPTER NINETEEN

After so much exuberant dancing, Ginger felt the need to soothe her throat with a drink of sparkling water. She returned to the table where she'd left her feather boa and her silver-studded handbag, and while partaking of the water found there, she spotted a small piece of plain white notepaper sticking out from underneath the clutch. Her skin grew cool as she read it.

Ginger scoured the room. Who could the messenger be?

Nancy Guilford was dancing with yet another new partner. Ginger had been so engrossed in her conversation with Basil Reed she hadn't noticed if Nancy Guilford stepped off the dance floor. It wouldn't have taken much for her to slip the note to Ginger on her way to visiting the ladies' room.

Other potentially guilty parties in the dance hall were Chief Officer MacIntosh, and Babineaux, who oversaw the refreshments. Mrs. Walsh, of course, was missing, as her presence as a recent widow would be scandalous. That didn't mean that she might not have taken a peek inside, possibly even asked one of the waiters to deliver the note for her.

As Ginger stood there considering, she felt as if she was being watched. Her first assumption was Basil Reed, but a glance in his direction saw him dancing with another woman, his attention fixed on her. Then her eyes landed back on Babineaux, who stared at her unabashedly. Was he signalling to her that he left the note?

She grabbed her clutch and made a trip to the lavatory. As she checked her hair and lipstick, she wondered how to get back into the pantry where the body was found. Ginger couldn't help feeling that she was missing an important piece to the puzzle. Maybe there was something she had missed. Everything had happened so fast on the day of the captain's murder, and the room had been full of people. If she could get in there to see it for herself without distraction, and let her mind work, maybe it would come to her. Ginger made her way to her table, but halfway there, she turned on her heel. Walking back to the ladies' room as if she had forgotten something, she made a detour just as she got to the door, and instead, exited the ballroom.

With the ball keeping most of the crew and staff occupied, Ginger sneaked to the kitchen below. When she reached the level of the pantries, it occurred to her that they might be locked. She came to the dry pantry first and checked the door. It opened easily, perhaps kept unlocked for convenience's sake. The door to the cool pantry was also unlocked. She flicked the light switch and stepped inside. Shivering, she hugged her boa and her clutch to her chest.

The near-empty shelves had only enough supplies to last one more day. Along the back were the barrels—the one where the captain was found was dismantled and set up against the wall. A string of rope marked off the crime scene. The scuff marks on the floor remained, but it wasn't clear if they belonged to the kitchen crew or to the intruders.

Ginger wasn't sure what she thought she might find there, but nothing obvious popped out. She turned away with a measure of disappointment. Heading to the door, she stuttered to a stop. The entrance was blocked.

Ginger took a step back, holding a hand to her heart. "Monsieur Babineaux, you frightened me."

Babineaux furrowed his bushy brows. "What are you doing here, Mrs. Gold?"

His dark eyes were fully dilated in the dim light, making him look sinister. Was Ginger looking into the black, beady eyes of a killer?

"I was just considering the case," she said. "I thought maybe I overlooked a clue in the pantry, but I've failed to discover anything new."

Babineaux took a step closer, further blocking her exit. Ginger was smart enough to feel a modicum of fear, but she wasn't going to let him know that. "Did you leave me the note?"

The cook's eyes flickered. "I know of no note."

Ginger stared back. He was either lying or protecting someone.

"It *ees* dangerous to wander around the ship alone, no?" Babineaux said. "You must be aware that you are trespassing."

The shadows from the nearby bulb cast eerie, ominous lines across Babineaux's face. Ginger regretted not putting her revolver in her clutch bag, though at the time she was getting ready for the dance, such precautions seemed unnecessary. If she was to die now at the hands of

Babineaux because she'd forgotten the revolver, Daniel would be so disappointed in her.

Ginger shaped her fingers and thumb to resemble a pistol and pressed them against her small handbag. She held Babineaux's gaze.

"I believe it is in your best interest to allow me to pass."

Babineaux's eyes flickered to her hand, his face registering understanding.

"You Americans think the answer for everything *ees* a gun."

"Sometimes it is."

Ginger's bluff worked, and Babineaux stepped aside. Ginger kept a wide berth, stayed out of arm's reach, and rushed down the corridor stairs.

CHAPTER TWENTY

Ginger hurried back to the upper deck, letting out a breath of relief as she got farther away from Babineaux. She'd checked over her shoulder several times to ensure he hadn't followed her.

Unlike when she'd left the ball to journey down to the pantry, passengers now filled the corridors and streamed past her. Had the dance ended already?

Ginger sensed there was something more drastic going on. The facial expressions weren't those of folks who'd just enjoyed a pleasant evening of dance, drink, and socialisation. Worry and distress seemed to weigh the crowd down. She observed Mr. and Mrs. Fairchild.

"What's happening?" Ginger asked them.

Mrs. Fairchild answered with high-pitched anxiety. "Officer MacIntosh put an end to the dance because we're heading into a storm. He wants everyone to return to their rooms. It's quite dreadful!"

Her husband reassured her. "Now, now, dear. The good fellow said it was just a precaution for our own safety." He looked at Ginger as if he feared he'd have to comfort another hysterical woman. "It's a light storm, soon to pass."

Ginger reined in her shock at hearing the man's voice. Things must be quite dire for him to feel the need to speak up.

"I'm sure you're right," Ginger said. Her stomach clenched at the news, and she wasted no time returning to Haley and Boss. Indeed, the wind had picked up tremendously, blowing ocean spray onto the outdoor corridor. Rain quickly grew from a drizzle to heavy droplets.

"You're back early," Haley said when Ginger arrived. "I thought these kinds of things went well into the wee hours of the morning." Then, before Ginger could respond, she stared at her soaked gown. "What happened to you?"

"Officer MacIntosh shut down the dance because of an imminent storm. It's pouring outside."

"Is it? I hadn't noticed."

That didn't surprise Ginger. Haley tuned out the world when she was lost in her studies.

Ginger removed her wet clothing and replaced her gown with a simple day dress. Though it was late enough to put on one's nightclothes, Ginger didn't feel it would be prudent with a storm brewing. One didn't know what would happen or whom one might meet.

"How bad is it?" Haley enquired.

"I wasn't actually in the ballroom when the announcement was made. I was informed by Mr. Fairchild that it's not serious, and everyone being sent to their rooms was just a precaution."

Haley lifted her chin. "Wouldn't want to risk anyone accidentally falling overboard."

Ginger checked the lock on the door to ensure it was

secure. "The storm could provide an opportunity for someone to dispose of an inconvenient acquaintance."

"Are you worried about your own safety?" Haley asked.

"It never hurts to be cautious. Something unnerving occurred this evening between myself and Babineaux."

Haley leaned forwards. "Do tell."

Ginger recounted the incident with the cook in the cool pantry.

"You should've come for me first," Haley said with a frown. "You could quite easily be shark food by now if he hadn't fallen for your pistol bluff."

"From what I could tell, the kitchen staff was occupied with the dance buffet," Ginger explained. "I honestly thought I could slip in, look around, and be out again in minutes. Babineaux must've been watching my movements and followed me."

"Highly suspicious."

Before Ginger could reply, the ship swayed, and Haley's books slid off the table. Boss's head perked up, and he let out a soft howl.

"It's okay, Bossy." Ginger placed him on her lap and snuggled his face, finding comfort in his soft fur.

Haley retrieved her books, returning them to the table just as the ship banked on the other side, sending her books in the other direction. "I think we should batten down the hatches," she said, collecting the stray books for a second time and locking them in one of the drawers in the sideboard. "At least the candlesticks are secured."

"Do you mind putting my shoes away?" Ginger said. "I don't want to let go of Boss."

Haley picked up the shoes and locked them in the wardrobe while stating, "Would hate to get hit in the head with one of these heels."

Again, the ship lurched sharply, and the tower of hat boxes in the corner tumbled over, showering Ginger's hats over the room. She cringed at the sight of all her beloved headwear strewn across the floor, unprotected. Before she could gather them up, the ship rocked violently again.

"Hang on!" Haley said.

Ginger held Boss tightly to her chest as she desperately clung to the brass railing that was secured to the wall.

The electric lights blew, casting them into darkness.

Oh, mercy!

The storm experience was reminiscent of her voyage in 1918 from Port du Le Havre to Boston Harbor. The ship had hit bad weather mid-Atlantic and tossed Ginger about her room, damaging her arm. She had been certain she was about to join her husband in heaven. Her stomach had heaved so mightily that she was thankful for the opportunity to act unladylike into a bucket. Thinking about it now made her brow break into a sweat. Ginger had faced many dangers in the past, but none frightened her as much as the thought of death by drowning.

"Are you all right?" Haley asked, bracing herself against the brass rail on the other side of the room.

"I will be. I just don't like the idea of perishing at sea."

"We're not going to per—" The bow raised sharply in a dangerous angle. Both Ginger and Haley lost their grip and were flung across the room. Fortunately, they rolled in the direction of the beds and crashed into their soft surfaces. Boss yelped as he fell to the floor.

"Boss!"

The ship levelled, allowing the poor hound to run to Ginger. If he'd had a tail, Ginger wouldn't doubt it would be situated between his legs in fear.

"Haley, if we die tonight, I want you to know I love you as a sister."

"Oh, Ginger. You know I feel the same, but we're not going to die."

"How do you know?"

"Gut feeling. Besides, we can't die without first clearing your name."

"So right, Nurse Higgins."

The storm persisted in its intensity for a good hour. Ginger's legs tired from constantly bracing herself, and she was grateful she hadn't eaten much that evening. No doubt there would be some unpleasant messes to clean up when this was over.

The wind and rain eventually eased, and Haley lit the candles. Ginger comforted Boss whilst greedily being comforted in return. She felt for Haley, who had no one to hold.

Ginger lifted Boss towards her. "Would you like a turn?"

Haley snorted lightly. "I'll pass." After helping Ginger collect her hats and deposit them back in their corresponding boxes, she returned her books to the table. "I guess I'll have to study by candlelight."

Ginger rested in her bed with Boss tucked in beside her, her mind a jumble of thoughts. She considered the revelation made by Chief Inspector Reed, and his suspicions about her personal life. Had the mystery attached to her name made her more of a suspect in the chief inspector's mind, or less so?

Then there was Babineaux—who now jumped to the top of the suspect list. He had motive and opportunity, but Ginger still lacked a reason for his keeping the corpse rather than disposing of it. Haley's suggestion that a crime mob might be involved had merit. It was quite possible that Babineaux needed to prove to someone that the death had occurred.

However, if that was the case, it didn't make sense why he'd reveal the body in the first place. Had he not pointed it out, everyone would've assumed the captain ended up overboard.

"I think I'm going to call it a night," Haley said as she closed her books and put her pencils away in a drawer. Ginger agreed and replaced her day dress with her night-clothes. After cleaning up in the lavatory, she tucked into bed. The ship's lurching calmed to a rhythmic rocking, and hopefully would help lull her to sleep.

Haley blew out the candles and said good night.

Ginger was about to respond in kind when she remembered.

"Haley, I almost forgot to tell you. Someone left me a note."

Ginger heard Haley shift her body weight to face her. "What did it say?"

"'If you know what's good for you, you'll mind your own business.'"

CHAPTER TWENTY-ONE

It was to Ginger's great relief that the storm abated overnight, and the sun once again broke through the clouds the next morning. Neither she nor Haley felt up to a full breakfast and decided a quiet morning inside was in order. They took a simple glass of orange juice with them to their room.

Ginger opted to keep Boss with her after their short visit to the kennel (which smelt worse than ever; her heart went out to the poor steerage folk). She explained to Scout, whom she was relieved to see had sustained himself through the storm, that Boss was fairly nervous as a result and should stay by her side for the day.

"Are you going to report your uncomfortable encounter with Babineaux to Chief Inspector Reed?" Haley asked.

"It occurred to me," Ginger admitted, "but in truth, I was the one in the wrong, having been found trespassing. Except for Babineaux's menacing body language—which I could've misinterpreted; the lighting in that room is terrible, and no doubt we both looked like ghouls—the cook never did anything untoward. I'm afraid the chief inspector would just give me one of his haughty looks, along with a lecture to leave the police work to him."

"Not bad advice," Haley said strongly. "If Babineaux is the killer, you really could be putting your life at risk."

Ginger agreed. "He's obviously quite smitten with Mrs. Walsh and seems compelled to protect her. Apparently, the captain could be quite wicked with his words."

"Babineaux wanting to release his lady love from distress is a powerful motive for murder."

Ginger gracefully crossed one leg over another. "Mrs. Walsh has her own motive."

"Right, the mistress."

"So sad to be locked in an unhappy marriage," Ginger said sombrely.

"Better to be single, I say," Haley replied. "So, where does this leave Nancy Guilford and Officer MacIntosh? They are in cahoots in some form or fashion. There's not a legitimate reason for him to be a guest in her private room."

"Miss Guilford and the first officer each have a potential motive for wanting the captain dead," Ginger said. "Perhaps with them it's a case of working together for a common goal, and not a lover's liaison."

"Well, if it's not the cook and the wife, then it's probably the actress and the officer."

"Unfortunately, we have no proof."

Haley nodded. "And time is ticking."

By noon, their stomachs felt a tad steadier, and they ventured towards the dining hall. Seamen continued to work vigorously to mop away standing water and ocean debris that the waves had flung on deck. Ginger and Haley clung to each other to prevent themselves from a fall on the slippery surface.

The hall was spectacularly empty, and Ginger didn't

doubt that many folk were still curled up in their beds recovering from the storm. After a light meal, Ginger collected Boss, and she and Haley joined a few other heartier travellers on the main deck, each claiming a free lounge chair to enjoy the sun. Ginger and Haley claimed a lounger, one next to the other, and Boss rested in the shade between them.

Ginger adjusted her grey straw hat, the wide brim pinned up at the front and decorated with two sprigs of imitation grapes. "I'm surprised you didn't vote to stay in the room to study."

"Even God took a day off."

"Oh, is it Sunday?"

Haley closed her eyes and tilted her chin to the rays. "It is to me."

As time went on, more passengers joined them for fresh air and sunshine after being holed up in their rooms during the storm. The women wore light cotton or rayon day frocks, with straw hats and white gloves. The men kept to light-coloured linen suits and matching flat linen caps. Well-dressed children held on to their mother's skirts, and Ginger spotted a small girl wearing a pretty chemise Jeanne Lanvin frock.

A man wearing a white shirt and thin black tie under a Fair Isle sweater slowed his pace as he walked by and tipped his hat at Ginger. She smiled and watched as he joined a woman reclining in a chair down the row.

"Men!" Haley spat. "That was an obvious pass at you, and he's got a lady waiting only a few yards away."

Ginger sobered. "All the good ones died in the war."

"Oh, honey, I'm sorry." Haley reached for Ginger's hand and squeezed. "I can be so thoughtless at times."

"It's quite all right. Now, where were we?"

"In the middle of solving a mystery."

"Yes. So much more fun than men."

Haley grinned, and Ginger laughed.

Elise Walsh eventually ventured out in her trademark black, narrow-waist dress suitable for a woman in mourning. Long black-lace gloves reached her elbows, and her eyes were partially hidden behind a black veil pinned to her short-brimmed hat.

Ginger noted with interest that Mrs. Walsh's cheeks sported a colour she hadn't had before. She whispered to Haley, "Mrs. Walsh is looking better than ever."

"You've heard the term, 'happy widow'?" Haley said.

Mrs. Walsh walked past Ginger and Haley without acknowledging them. Ginger was just about to call out, when Nancy Guilford turned the corner onto the lounge deck and nearly ran head-on into Elise Walsh. The heat of bitterness flashed between them, and Ginger worried that if they had been men and not refined women, a fistfight might've broken out.

Mrs. Walsh skirted around Nancy in a self-righteous huff, while Nancy's stare was like a knife blade to the widow's back.

"No love lost there," Haley said after a moment.

Ginger agreed. "One probably suspects the other."

"One is probably right."

CHAPTER TWENTY-TWO

Nancy Guilford took up a position at the rail looking out to sea. She fished out a cigarette—not bothering with a holder—lit the tip and inhaled deeply. She released a puff of smoke through her bright red, lipstick-laden lips and promptly inhaled again. Ginger thought this an indication that Nancy Guilford's encounter with Mrs. Walsh unnerved her.

Ginger tugged on Boss's leash as she got to her feet. She nodded towards the actress and Haley followed.

"Hello," Ginger called out.

Nancy Guilford eyed Ginger and Haley cautiously as they approached. "Hello, ladies, how are ya?"

"Terrific," Ginger said. "Such a lovely day."

"Especially after yesterday's storm," Nancy said. "Poor Patty was in the toilet the whole time, emptying her stomach."

"Beyond that unfortunate patch of weather, it's been a particularly pleasant summer," Haley said. "I'm happy to have escaped the humidity."

"You can say that again," Nancy said as she released

another puff of smoke "Which is why I so much prefer the West Coast. Los Angeles has delightfully dry summers."

"What brings you to England?" Ginger asked.

"My agent wants to introduce me to an important playwright. He believes I would be perfect for the lead in an upcoming production."

Ginger found that hard to imagine with the calf-like sound of the actress's voice, but said, "Sounds exciting."

Nancy shrugged and let her cigarette fall into the ocean. "It's work."

Patty approached, still looking a tad green around the gills. "Here's your coffee, Miss Guilford," she said, handing Nancy a mug. Nancy took it without a word of thanks, and Ginger wondered what she had on Patty Applebalm that she could get the older woman to wait on her hand and foot like that.

Patty waited for further instructions, and when none came, settled herself onto one of the lounge chairs.

Ginger lowered her voice. "Has Patty been with you long?"

"Oh, Patty?" Nancy glanced at her assistant. "Sure. She's a trouper. No family to speak of, so I never have to worry about her ditchin' me. I treat her decent-like, ya know. For a woman her age, there ain't a lot of good jobs around."

Nancy Guilford had her story down when it came to her pseudo-relationship with her aunt.

"I'm certain she is quite in your debt," Ginger said.

Nancy's eyes flashed with something hard to define before she changed the subject. "What are you gals gonna do in England? Gonna take in any theatre? I hear they've got some great plays."

"No, nothing so exciting as that," Ginger said. She

recounted her father's passing and her subsequent need to handle the estate, and Haley's entry into medical school.

"Wowza," Nancy said loudly. "A lady doctor! I'm impressed." Ginger believed Nancy to be sincere in her proclamation because her thinly veiled interest in the plainer woman disappeared. She now considered Haley with real admiration.

"Could I enquire," Ginger said, "has Chief Chief Inspector Reed given you any clue as to who might be behind the captain's death? Or who might be behind the blackmail?"

Nancy stiffened at the question, then fell into her role play and smiled. "No, but I wish he would. And ain't he just the most dashing man! I promised to meet up with him in London for drinks."

The thought of Basil Reed seeing Nancy Guilford socially did something strange to Ginger's stomach, but she ignored it and pressed on. "I'm sure he'll show you a good time."

A late afternoon breeze stirred, tangling loose strands of Nancy's golden hair. "It's been nice chatting, but I need to get out of the wind." She motioned to Patty. "A scarf."

Patty peeled herself off the chair and returned to Nancy, carrying a leather satchel. As Nancy began to walk away, Patty reached into the bag to retrieve a colourful silk scarf. She passed it to Nancy, who pulled it over her head and tied it underneath her chin. She finger-waved with long, delicate fingers. "See ya around!"

Ginger and Haley watched them go.

"Interesting," Haley said.

Boss stretched out on his leash and sniffed at a small object on the deck floor. Ginger hurried to examine the item and picked it up. "Good boy, Boss."

"What is it?" Haley asked.

"It must've caught on Nancy's scarf." Ginger held up a lone cuff link, its fleur de lis insignia flashing in the rays of the setting sun. "I think I know who the killer couple is."

CHAPTER TWENTY-THREE

Ginger had an idea, relayed it to Haley, and they parted ways. Ginger dropped Boss off at her room, then headed back to the starboard corridor and knocked on Miss Guilford's door. As if she was expecting company, Nancy Guilford opened it, her expression of glee slipping into dismay. She wore a slinky dress and held two empty champagne flutes.

"Celebrating?" Ginger said. She didn't wait to be invited in and pushed herself past the actress.

"Hey, wait a minute. You got no right to barge in here like that."

"Who are you waiting for?" Ginger countered. "Your partner in crime?"

Nancy fell into the role of an innocent. "I have no idea what you're talking about." She put the flutes down on the sideboard and lit up a cigarette, this time using an ebony holder. She slid languidly into a chair, crossing long legs.

"Have I mentioned I'm a big fan of yours," Ginger said. "I've seen all your films." Nancy perked up a little at that.

"As a courtesy and because I'm such a big fan, I thought

I should tell you..." She held out the sentence until she was certain she had Nancy's attention.

"Tell me what?" Nancy prompted impatiently.

"I thought you should know that Mrs. Elise Walsh has implicated you for the murder of her husband."

Nancy blew out a puff of air. "Well, that's not so astonishing, is it? Of course, the wife would accuse the mistress."

"She says she has proof."

For the first time, Nancy looked troubled. Her eyelashes fluttered. "She's bluffing."

Ginger noticed the door to the adjoining room had slid open a crack since they arrived and wasn't surprised when the eavesdropper slipped in.

"Hello, Miss Applebalm."

Patty pinned Ginger with a steely gaze, but spoke to Nancy. "Is everything all right, Miss Guilford?"

"Everything's hunky-dory, Patty. Mrs. Gold was just leaving."

"Suit yourself," Ginger said casually. "Forewarned is forearmed, you know."

By the time she got to the door, someone knocked on the other side. "Chief Officer MacIntosh! Fancy meeting you here."

MacIntosh's eyes darted from Ginger to Nancy, and Nancy just shrugged. "She showed up uninvited."

"Is this another example of your courtesy?" Ginger said. "Making sure a passenger is comfortable? I'm still waiting for a visit from you, in that case." She folded her arms. "In fact, I'm growing more and more 'uncomfortable'."

MacIntosh straightened and called on the authority of his position to excuse himself. "Miss Guilford, would you like to accompany me to... somewhere else, where we may discuss matters in private?"

She stamped out her cigarette in a large porcelain ashtray and jumped to her feet. "Yes, please."

"But, Officer MacIntos—" Ginger started.

He pointed a thick finger in her direction. "I don't have to justify my actions and whereabouts to you, Mrs. Gold." Just as he reached for the knob, there was another knock.

"Is there a party scheduled in my room today that I didn't know about?" Nancy said. The door opened to Mrs. Walsh. Her bloodshot eyes and the fiery redness in her cheeks spoke volumes. She was unable to compose herself, even after registering that Nancy Guilford wasn't alone.

"Are you quite all right, Mrs. Walsh?" MacIntosh said.

"What are you doing here?" Nancy said.

Elise Walsh glared at Nancy and hissed, "We need to speak in private."

"Why? So you can accuse me of murder?"

Mrs. Walsh stepped across the room. "Like you accused me?"

Haley had delivered the same message to Elise Walsh as Ginger had relayed to Nancy Guilford, planting the accusation from one to the other.

Nancy shouted. "I didn't accuse you!"

"Ladies, ladies," Ginger said. "Perhaps I can help." She produced the cuff link, and silence fell as everyone stared at it. "This dropped onto the deck, Miss Guilford, when Miss Applebalm removed your scarf from her bag. It belonged to Captain Walsh."

MacIntosh's eyes locked on Nancy Guilford.

"It's no secret I was involved with the captain," Nancy said defensively.

"Mrs. Walsh, I believe you have the other one?" Ginger said.

"So? Why wouldn't I have my own husband's cuff links?"

"Ah, well, you did have both of them, didn't you? You'd taken them from your husband's dressing table so that he couldn't wear them again."

"Why would I do that?" Mrs. Walsh said bitterly.

"Because you knew they were given to him as a gift from Miss Guilford. It was why he said they had sentimental value."

Nancy gulped. "How do you know that?"

Ginger opened a sideboard drawer and removed a receipt. "A silver set of cuff links with the fleur de lis engraved, purchased recently from the Boston Jewelers Exchange."

Nancy's full mouth tightened.

"I managed a little peek when we came to visit," Ginger explained. "You really should close your drawers properly when company calls."

Nancy grumbled and folded her arms over her chest. "It was a wasted effort on my part to get him to leave the witch, but I didn't kill him."

Ginger turned to Patty Applebalm. "You love your niece deeply, don't you? She's all you have left of your beloved sister." Then she repeated the words Mrs. Fairchild had said earlier. "You'd do *anything* for Nancy, wouldn't you?"

Nancy sat up. Her eyes found Patty Applebalm's, and the room seemed to still. She shook her head. "No, no, it's not what you think."

Ginger cocked her head and held up the cuff link. "Isn't it?"

Miss Applebalm pointed a finger at Elise Walsh. "She struck him first!"

"Patty!" Nancy's face was now an unflattering shade of red. "Shut up!"

"'Struck him first'?" Chief Inspector Reed's voice came from the open doorway. "Does that mean that you hit him the second time, Miss Applebalm?"

Ginger looked to Haley, who stood at the doorway, and gave her a thumbs-up sign. But, in the next instant, Patty Applebalm was behind Ginger, and she whipped Nancy's colourful silk scarf around her neck.

Patty Applebaum's voice trembled as she shouted, "Everyone out, or I'll hurt her!"

CHAPTER TWENTY-FOUR

Chief Inspector Reed held both hands up. "Now, just hold on there."

"Auntie," Nancy said, clearly shaken. "You're not thinking straight. Release Mrs. Gold, and we'll talk about this rationally."

Patty shook her head sharply. "Neither you nor I will go to jail for that horrid man. Nor for his wicked, stupid wife!"

"Patty, please," Nancy pleaded. "This isn't the way."

"What other way is there?" she spat back. "He dishonoured you and the child."

Nancy's eyes popped with disbelief. "Patty!"

"It's true, they might as well know now. That despicable man didn't even have the decency to take care of his own flesh and blood. He left them to fend for themselves."

Elise Walsh collapsed against the sideboard. "I knew it!"

Nancy Guilford sank into her chair. Her secret was out. Ginger felt for her—unwed and unsupported, worried for the welfare of her child. No wonder she and the captain had words.

"Were you blackmailing Captain Walsh, Miss Applebalm?" Ginger asked. Though the scarf was snug around Ginger's neck, she wasn't in too much discomfort. She was willing to wait it out to get the full confession.

"I was and didn't feel one bit bad for it. It was the only way to give the child a chance at a decent life. My niece might act rich, but believe me, it's all a show. She gets paid a pittance."

Nancy let out a low, spirit-wounded moan.

Patty Applebalm's voice pitched higher. "He threatened to go to the police and confess all, to expose us. I went to his room to confront him, and when Mrs. Walsh found us together..." Patty laughed maniacally. "She hit him out of jealousy. Jealousy! Can you believe that? As if I'd let that man touch a hair on my head! I just finished off what she started."

"It was the last straw!" Elise Walsh bellowed. "I wouldn't stand for another speck of humiliation from my husband, whatever his reason for allowing you, you insipid cow, into his room."

As if she was having an out-of-body experience, Ginger saw the scene from an objective stance. Defeated, Nancy slumped in the chair like a rag doll. Elise Walsh stood to the side and twitched like a trapped animal. The chief inspector and Haley blocked the door, calculating their next move as they watched Ginger and her captor. MacIntosh's eyes darted from person to person, arms forward as if he could keep things from spiralling out of control with his mind.

Ginger had been in life-threatening situations before. France, in 1917, had been a place of constant fear. Her missions were dangerous, but she'd been trained to keep her cool. She had learned to gauge her odds in any given situation and discern the best move to keep her and those around her alive. In this situation, Ginger was the only one in any kind of imminent danger. Her throat burned in her effort to breathe, and stars formed around the edges of her vision.

Ginger wondered whether Patty Applebalm knew the penalty for murder in England was hanging.

Miss Applebalm, sensing her own desperate position, shouted, "Get out!" She tightened the scarf around Ginger's neck.

Ginger struggled, grabbing at her throat.

Haley panicked. "Do as she says!" She stepped backwards towards the door. Chief Inspector Reed took a step towards Ginger just as Elise Walsh made a beeline for the door, but he caught her by the arm and held fast. Patty's eyes were pinned on the activity as the chief inspector quickly clamped handcuffs on her nemesis.

Taking advantage of her captor's distraction, Ginger swiftly elbowed Patty Applebaum in the stomach. Patty folded with a gasp, loosening her hold on Ginger. Ginger released the scarf from her neck and used it to bind Patty Applebalm's hands behind her back.

Ginger looked over at Basil Reed and smiled. "I'm so glad you could make it, Chief Inspector."

CHAPTER TWENTY-FIVE

Ginger presumed Elise Walsh's guilt, but she wasn't sure until the end whether Nancy Guilford had covered for Patty Applebalm or the other way around. When Mrs. Fairchild insisted that Miss Applebalm would do *anything* for Nancy, Ginger had wondered if that included murder. Turned out it did.

Mrs. Walsh feared the captain's last will and testament would be void without a body, or at the very least its execution much delayed, and to support her future, she was relying on being the sole benefactor. With the help of the food trolley the captain had ordered for his liaison with Miss Guilford, the two women managed to get the man down to the pantry and into the near-empty pickle barrel, where his body would be preserved. Elise Walsh gave Patty Applebalm one of the fleur de lis cuff links as a sign of the short-lived pact between them. It was just bad luck that Babineaux had stumbled on the corpse so quickly.

Ginger made a trip to steerage to recover Boss from the kennel.

"Dear Scout," she said as the boy handed her pet over.

"Thanks so much for taking care of Boss, and for your discretion in the other matter."

"'Tis fine, missus. Me and your Boss got along real well. I'll miss the ol' feller."

"I'm sure he'll miss you, too." The emotion Ginger felt saying goodbye surprised her. "Are you staying in London? Surely you must attend school somewhere?"

"There's nuffin' I need learnin' that my cousin Marvin can't teach me."

Ginger wanted to snatch the eager-faced boy and run. Before she could think it through, she said, "You could come live with me if you like. You'd have a safe home and learn to properly read and write."

"Aw, missus, I couldn't. My cousin needs me. And it ain't my place in this world to be wiv grand folks like yerself. Anyways, I 'ave me ol' uncle to fink about."

Ginger sighed. She had no business trying to swoop in and rescue Scout like he was a stray puppy. He had a family, and besides, she wasn't even planning on staying in London. What was she going to do? Steal him off to Boston?

"I understand perfectly. I do hope we will meet again sometime in the future."

"Yes, missus. That'd be brilliant."

Ginger affectionately patted the boy on the head, then tugged on Boss's leash. She made a point to smile at all the steerage folk on the way out.

Doing something for the last time, even a simple and mundane thing like picking up her dog from steerage, squeezed Ginger's heart. Walking the open deck of first class, breathing in the saline air, and watching the bow of the *Rosa* cutting through the cool waters of the Atlantic, all for the final time on this trip. In the distance she could see a sliver of brown on the horizon—land. She took a second to enjoy the beauty. One thing Ginger had learned well was not to take the future for granted and to make the most of each moment, firmly grounded in the present.

"Mrs. Gold!"

Ginger snapped out of her reverie at the sound of Roy Hardy's voice. "Hello, Mr. Hardy!"

He raced down the deck and was red in the face from exertion and, Ginger presumed, excitement. "It worked! Your plan worked! Miss Chloe smiled and invited me to eat lunch with her, and now we've made plans to meet up for drinks in Liverpool!"

Ginger clapped her hands. "I'm so happy for you, Mr. Hardy, and I'm not surprised. You're a great catch!"

"You're too kind, madam."

"*Pfft*. It's true. And do visit me in London if you ever find yourself there." Ginger didn't know why she extended the invitation. She was sincere in her desire to see the young man and his sweetheart again, but unless they visited in the next month or so, she would have left for America.

He shook her hand with exuberant gratitude, and then hurriedly returned to whatever chore he'd interrupted when he beheld her.

When Ginger rounded the corner towards her room, she recognised Miss Guilford staring mournfully out to sea. Her arms were crossed over a turquoise floral day frock that had a wide white sailor collar that draped over her shoulders. A wide-brimmed hat decorated with a long white-satin ribbon, shaded her eyes from the glare of the sun that lowered in the west.

"Miss Guilford," Ginger called out. "Are you all right?"

"Right as rain, honey," she said without a smile. Ginger noted the sarcasm.

"I am very sorry for all that has happened."

"Patty was just a meddling middle-aged woman who only thought of herself." Nancy Guilford spoke forcefully, but the lone tear that escaped gave away the affection she felt for her aunt.

But Ginger couldn't disagree with Nancy's harsh words. Patty had been blackmailing the captain over his bastard child, which was why he'd borrowed money from Ginger's father, money Ginger didn't know if she'd ever see again.

"She was misguided and disturbed, I'll give you that," Ginger said. "But I know she means a lot to you."

"How would you know that?" Nancy scowled. "You don't know me at all!"

Ginger held the photo of the infant she'd been carrying in her pocket. "I believe this belongs to you."

Nancy's fingers trembled as she took it. "Where did you find it?"

Ginger wasn't about to give her means and methods away, so instead of answering said, "You spoke truthfully about being in the captain's room the night he died, but you weren't there as his guest. Rather, your aunt had told you what she'd done. You went there for the murder weapon and then threw it overboard, didn't you? To protect her. It's why it hasn't been found."

Nancy stared at her with sad and forlorn eyes, but said nothing. Her silence confirmed Ginger's conviction to the truth. That and the "big ol' floppy 'at" on Nancy's head, unlike anything Patty or Elise Walsh had ever worn.

CHAPTER TWENTY-SIX

There was just enough time left to pack up before the SS *Rosa* was scheduled to dock in Liverpool. Ginger had booked a room at an inn for herself and Haley, and the two of them would take the train into London the next day.

"Do you need any more help?" Haley offered. Her two suitcases had been packed and ready for some time.

Ginger's trunks and suitcases were filled and her hat boxes stacked. "I think not. The porter should be here shortly for my luggage."

"Will someone be waiting for us when we arrive at Hartigan House?" Haley asked. "Or are we about to present ourselves to an empty place?"

"You know," Ginger said, "I'm not sure. Besides Pips, whatever staff there is at Hartigan House will have been hired by Father, or perhaps by Pips himself."

"Who's Pips?"

"Clive Pippins is the butler. He's been on at Hartigan House since I was a child." Ginger's mind pulled up pleasant memories of the friendly man. "I always called him Pips, and he called me 'little miss.' It's been two decades since I've seen him. I was heartbroken when my father made me say goodbye."

"A happy reunion, then," Haley said.

"I'm sure."

Haley stared out the small window. "I'm going a bit stir-crazy waiting." She turned and stared at the dog. "Why don't I take the boss for a walk?"

"Good idea," Ginger said. She wouldn't mind a few moments alone.

Once Haley and Boss left, Ginger inhaled deeply and embraced the peace and quiet. She emptied the final item from the drawer of her night table—a black-and-white photo of a handsome Royal Army Service Corps officer in uniform.

"My dearest lieutenant, I'm almost there."

Ginger lightly kissed the photograph before slipping it into her handbag.

There was a soft tapping on the door, and to Ginger's surprise, Basil Reed was on the other side of the threshold.

"Chief Inspector," Ginger said with a smile.

"Please, do call me Basil."

"Basil. Come in. And you must call me Ginger."

"Ginger? Is that a nickname?"

"It is. I was named Georgia after my father George, but my mother called me Ginger." She tapped her bob. "Because of my hair. She said one George in the family was enough."

Basil smiled. "I like it."

"I wish I could offer you something to drink, but alas, everything has been packed up."

"That's quite all right. I can't stay long. I just wanted to say, um, well, thank you for your help today. I'm not sure I would've solved the case before docking without your assistance."

"You're welcome. Besides the slight choking incident at the end, I quite enjoyed myself."

"Right. That was a particularly unpleasant moment for me as well. I also came to give you this." He took another step towards Ginger and handed her a folded piece of paper. "The concierge was on his way to deliver it, and I said I'd be happy to run the errand for him."

"A telegram?"

"Yes. I'll go now and let you read it in privacy." He held out a hand. "Perhaps we'll meet again in London sometime."

"That would be delightful."

As soon as the chief inspector closed the door behind him, Ginger opened the telegram.

GHASTLY DISCOVERY IN ATTIC OF HARTIGAN HOUSE STOP AWAIT YOUR ARRIVAL FOR ADVICE STOP PIPPINS

~

Don't miss *Murder at Hartigan House*.
Read on for an excerpt.

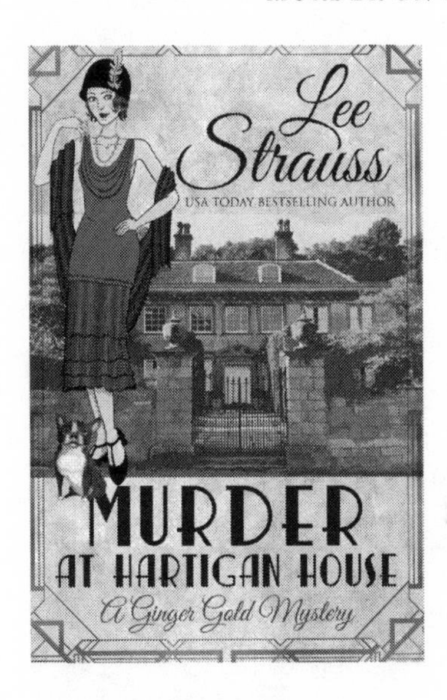

There's a skeleton in the attic!

After a weeklong passage over the Atlantic from Boston to Liverpool, Ginger Gold arrives at her childhood London home—Hartigan House—to find decade-old remains from some poor woman on the floor in the attic. Ginger's Boston terrier, Boss, noses out a missing phalange from under the bed.

It's a mystery that once again puts Ginger alongside the handsome Chief Inspector Basil Reed. Who is the victim? And how did she end up in Ginger's home?

Clues lead Ginger and her good friend Haley Higgins to a soirée hosted in 1913 by Ginger's late father, George Hartigan. A shadow of suspicion is cast on her father's legacy, and Ginger isn't so sure she wants to know the truth about the man she dearly loved.

Ginger decides to host another soirée, inviting the guest list from ten years previous. Before the night is over, another person is dead.

On AMAZON!

Go to **leestraussbooks.com** to sign up for Lee's READERS' LIST and gain access to Ginger Gold's private Journal. Find out about Ginger's Life before the SS *Rosa* and how she became the woman she has. This is a fluid document that will cover her romance with her late husband Daniel, her time serving in the British secret service during World War One, and beyond. Includes a recipe for Dark Dutch Chocolate Cake!

It begins: **July 31, 1912**

How fabulous that I found this Journal today, hidden in the bottom of my wardrobe. Good old Pippins, our English butler in London, gave it to me as a parting gift when Father whisked me away on our American adventure so he could marry Sally. Pips said it was for me to record my new adventures. I'm ashamed I never even penned one word before today. I think I was just too sad.

This old leather-bound journal takes me back to that emotional time. I had shed enough tears to fill the ocean and I remember telling Father dramatically that I was certain to cause flooding to match God's. At eight years old I was well-trained in my biblical studies, though, in retro-spect, I would say that I had probably bordered on heresy with my little tantrum.

The first week of my "adventure" was spent with a tummy ache and a number of embarrassing sessions that involved a bucket and Father holding back my long hair so I wouldn't soil it with vomit.

I certainly felt that I was being punished for some reason. Hartigan House—though large and sometimes lonely—was my home and Pips was my good friend. He often helped me to pass the time with games of I Spy and Xs and Os.

"Very good, Little Miss," he'd say with a twinkle in his blue eyes when I won, which I did often. I suspect now that our good butler wasn't beyond letting me win even when unmerited.

Father had got it into his silly head that I needed a mother, but I think the truth was he wanted a wife. Sally, a woman half my father's age, turned out to be a sufficient wife in the end, but I could never claim her as a mother.

Well, Pips, I'm sure you'd be happy to know that things turned out all right here in America.

Subscribe to read more!
www.leestraussbooks.com/join-ginger

Ginger Gold has her own website!

GingerGoldMysteries.com
Check it out!

ABOUT THE AUTHOR

Lee Strauss is a USA TODAY bestselling author of The Ginger Gold Mysteries series, The Higgins & Hawke Mystery series, The Rosa Reed Mystery series (cozy historical mysteries), A Nursery Rhyme Mystery series (mystery suspense), The Perception series (young adult dystopian), The Light & Love series (sweet romance), The Clockwise Collection (YA time travel romance), and young adult historical fiction with over a million books read. She has titles published in German, Spanish and Korean, and a growing audio library.

When Lee's not writing or reading she likes to cycle, hike, and stare at the ocean. She loves to drink caffè lattes and red wines in exotic places, and eat dark chocolate anywhere.

For more info on books by Lee Strauss and her social media links, visit leestraussbooks.com. To make sure you don't miss the next new release, be sure to sign up for her readers' list!

Discuss the books, ask questions, share your opinions. Fun giveaways! Join the Lee Strauss Readers' Group on Facebook for more info.

Love the fashions of the 1920s? Check out Ginger Gold's Pinterest Board!

Did you know you can follow your favourite authors on Bookbub? If you subscribe to Bookbub — (and if you don't, why don't you? - They'll send you daily emails alerting you to sales and new releases on just the kind of books you like to read!) — follow me to make sure you don't miss the next Ginger Gold Mystery!

www.leestraussbooks.com
leestraussbooks@gmail.com

MORE FROM LEE STRAUSS

On AMAZON

GINGER GOLD MYSTERY SERIES (cozy 1920s historical)

Cozy. Charming. Filled with Bright Young Things. This Jazz Age murder mystery will entertain and delight you with its 1920s flair and pizzazz!

Murder on the SS Rosa

Murder at Hartigan House

Murder at Bray Manor

Murder at Feathers & Flair

Murder at the Mortuary

Murder at Kensington Gardens

Murder at St. George's Church

The Wedding of Ginger & Basil

Murder Aboard the Flying Scotsman

Murder at the Boat Club

Murder on Eaton Square

Murder by Plum Pudding

Murder on Fleet Street

Murder at Brighton Beach

Murder in Hyde Park

Murder at the Royal Albert Hall

Murder in Belgravia

Murder on Mallowan Court

Murder at the Savoy

Murder at the Circus

Murder at the Boxing Club

Murder in France

LADY GOLD INVESTIGATES (Ginger Gold companion short stories)

Volume 1

Volume 2

Volume 3

Volume 4

HIGGINS & HAWKE MYSTERY SERIES (cozy 1930s historical)

The 1930s meets Rizzoli & Isles in this friendship depression era cozy mystery series.

Death at the Tavern

Death on the Tower

Death on Hanover

Death by Dancing

THE ROSA REED MYSTERIES

(1950s cozy historical)

Murder at High Tide

Murder on the Boardwalk

Murder at the Bomb Shelter

Murder on Location

Murder and Rock 'n Roll

Murder at the Races

Murder at the Dude Ranch

Murder in London

Murder at the Weddings

A NURSERY RHYME MYSTERY SERIES(mystery/sci fi)

Marlow finds himself teamed up with intelligent and savvy Sage Farrell, a girl so far out of his league he feels blinded in her presence - literally - damned glasses! Together they work to find the identity of @gingerbreadman. Can they stop the killer before he strikes again?

Gingerbread Man

Life Is but a Dream

Hickory Dickory Dock

Twinkle Little Star

LIGHT & LOVE (sweet romance)

Set in the dazzling charm of Europe, follow Katja, Gabriella, Eva, Anna and Belle as they find strength, hope and love.

Sing me a Love Song

Your Love is Sweet

In Light of Us

Lying in Starlight

PLAYING WITH MATCHES (WW2 history/romance)

A sobering but hopeful journey about how one young German boy copes with the war and propaganda. Based on true events.

A Piece of Blue String (companion short story)

THE CLOCKWISE COLLECTION (YA time travel romance)

Casey Donovan has issues: hair, height and uncontrollable trips to the 19th century! And now this ~ she's accidentally taken Nate Mackenzie, the cutest boy in the school, back in time. Awkward.

Clockwise

Clockwiser

Like Clockwork

Counter Clockwise

Clockwork Crazy

Clocked (companion novella)

Standalones

Seaweed

Love, Tink

MURDER AT HARTIGAN HOUSE

CHAPTER ONE

Ginger Gold hesitated at the front door of Hartigan House. She hadn't expected to feel anything, but instead she shouldered a heavy shawl of melancholy. This grand, three-story structure built of limestone, situated in the picturesque Kensington Street of Mallowan Court, had grown tired over the war years, the stones grayer, the garden wilder. The house had been her home for the first eight years of her life. The last time she'd visited had been a decade earlier, on her honeymoon.

Her mostly happy childhood was long gone, as was her lovely husband.

Haley Higgins, Ginger's good friend and traveling companion, noticed her disquietude. "Is everything all right?"

"Hartigan House holds a lot of memories." Ginger was torn in her allegiances: London, the place of her birth, or Boston, the place where she came of age. She'd lived in the brownstone on Beacon Hill for over twenty-two years, yet England was etched deeply in her soul.

And now, to finally return—it was with this disconcerting welcome. A telegram received while on board the SS *Rosa*: GHASTLY DISCOVERY IN ATTIC OF HARTIGAN HOUSE.

Ginger, rousing her inner strength, stepped to the front door and engaged the wrought-iron knocker.

"This is your house, isn't it?" Haley said. A lock of long, curly brown hair escaped its faux bob, and she pushed it behind her ear. "Surely you don't have to knock?"

"I'm not in possession of a key, and I'm quite certain the door is locked."

Haley tested the knob and found Ginger's prediction to be true.

Ginger adjusted her yellow cloche hat, trimmed with blue ribbon to match her fine linen suit purchased on Fifth Avenue in New York, and patted her red bob with gloved hands. Her Boston terrier, Boss, waited obediently by her feet.

Their arrival was expected. Ginger had telegrammed the details of her journey before leaving Boston, and the door soon opened. Standing before them was Mr. Pippins, the butler. The years seemed to have caught up with him. His shoulders slumped slightly, and his hair had all but disappeared. But his eyes remained their bright cornflower blue, and they twinkled as he stared back at her.

"My dear Lady Gold." He spoke her name with a slight quiver, giving away the emotion he experienced at seeing her. A dramatic image flashed through Ginger's mind: a scrawny redheaded girl held firmly by her father's strong hands as she wept, her eyes locking with her beloved butler as her father took her away.

A tear escaped from the corner of her eye, and she threw herself into his arms. "Oh, Pips."

Clive Pippins, stiffening at first to this unorthodox

greeting, returned the embrace. Ginger released her hold, stepped back, and clasped her hands in front of her. She sensed Pippins's embarrassment and shared in it. There were proper ways to do things, especially in England, and showing overt affection to a member of one's staff was *not* proper. She cleared her throat and smiled. "It's so good to see you again, Pips."

Pippins stood tall, hands relaxed behind his back. "My sympathies, once again, on the loss of your father. Mr. Hartigan was a good man."

"Thank you." Ginger desperately missed her father, but seeing Pippins and knowing his devotion to her helped to ease some of the pain.

Ginger glanced at Haley, who stood expectantly in her brown tweed suit and sturdy Oxford heels. "Oh, my manners. Pippins, this is my good friend, Miss Higgins."

Pippins bowed. "Madam."

"How do you do, Mr. Pippins," Haley said with her noticeable Boston accent. She reached out her hand, her eyes crinkling at the corners as she smiled. "I'm a commoner."

Pippins's lips twitched in amusement. He accepted her hand with a sturdy shake.

"Miss Higgins was Father's nurse for the last three years," Ginger said. "She's come to London to study at the London School of Medicine for Women." Ginger linked her arm to Haley's. "She's going to be a doctor!"

Pippins nodded agreeably. "How wonderful."

Ginger swooped up her Boston terrier and patted his black head affectionately. "And this is Boss. Short for Boston."

"A fine-looking specimen, madam. How was your journey?"

"Quite lovely," Ginger said. "Apart from a short but fierce storm, the weather was pleasant." She omitted the news about the murder onboard the SS *Rosa* and the part she and Haley played in solving it.

Ginger finally had a chance to take in the foyer. Black-and-white-tiled floor, a large chandelier that hung from the height of the second level, windows on either side of the double-paneled front doors that added natural light. The formidable Areca palm plants in large ceramic pots hailing from India, once lined up along the base of the stairwell, were missing—much to be expected when a house has been shut up for so many years.

"We don't have a footman, madam," Pippins said, "but I'd be happy to bring your things in."

Pippins, a confirmed bachelor, had to be in his seventies now, and Ginger didn't intend to burden him with such a laborious task. "That's quite all right, Pips. I've arranged for our things to be transported here by motor van. The driver will be able to manage."

"Yes, madam."

Ginger eyed him wistfully. "I don't suppose you could call me 'Little Miss'?" Little Miss had been Pippins's pet name for her when she was a child. He was the only staff member to take time to entertain her. Subtle games like I Spy and Noughts and Crosses (what Haley would call X's and O's)—never when her father was around, or in the presence of other staff, as that would be unseemly for a member of the staff. Her heart squeezed with the nostalgia.

"'Little Miss,' madam?" His eyes flickered with the memory, and he smiled. "I think not, madam."

Ginger let out a playful sigh. The pet name didn't suit a thirty-year-old woman anyway.

"Can I bring you some tea, madam?" Pippins asked. "After the train ride from Liverpool, you must be worn out."

"Tea sounds marvelous, Pips, but first we must know what your urgent, mysterious message is all about," she said, referring to the telegram. Her curiosity was greater than her desire to put her feet up. Besides, she'd had a good sleep at the inn they'd stayed at overnight in Liverpool, and she currently didn't feel all that tired. "I take it you've found something distasteful?"

"I believe he used the word 'ghastly'," Haley said. "Such a strong word. I'm dying to know what it is."

Pippins's expression turned grave. "It *is* rather ghastly, so do prepare yourself. Please follow me." A wide staircase circled up to the second floor, which horseshoed around the foyer, giving the entrance its grand high ceiling. At the end of the passage was a door used by the servants to access the second floor. It opened to a small landing with steep steps that went down to the kitchen and up to the attic, where the staff sleeping quarters were found. Rooms for women were in the West wing, and the men's rooms to the east.

"I do apologize for bringing you into the servants' quarters, madam."

"It's quite all right, Pips."

Ginger's hope was that the problem in the attic was something trivial, like dry rot or black mould. She wondered why Pippins hadn't taken it upon himself to ring for repairs. Perhaps, since he was newly back to Hartigan House and answered now to her instead of her father, he no longer felt he had the authority to make such calls on his own.

"I'm filled with curiosity, Pippins," Ginger said. "Do give us a clue."

Pippins hesitated, then said. "I'm really at a loss how to describe it."

"Can we pause for a breather?" Haley said, stopping midway up the step. "I am out of shape."

"I'm no better," Ginger said. "Pippins is bringing us to shame."

Pippins puffed out his chest with pride. "Years of going up and down daily, madam."

Ginger laughed. "Perhaps we should take rooms up here, Haley."

Pippins instantly turned serious. "Absolutely not, madam."

Before Ginger could explain that she wasn't serious, Pippins marched down the passage in the men's quarters to the very last room at the end. He removed a key from his pocket. "A skeleton key, madam," he explained. "Opens all the attic doors."

The lock clicked, and the door swung open.

As Ginger reached the threshold, she couldn't keep a gasp of horror from escaping her lips.

Oh, mercy!

In the middle of the room, lying on the floor, was a decomposed body.

ACKNOWLEDGMENTS

Many thanks go to my editors, Angelika Offenwanger and Robbi Brandt, and to my early readers, especially Caroline Andrews for helping me get young Scout's slang and accent right, and Heather Belleguelle for helping me nab those errant typo gremlins, and stay true to the era and British culture.

A big shout-out to my review crew for keeping the reviews coming, and to my Facebook readers' group for reading my books and hanging out with me online.

I don't know how I did it before Shadi Bleiken came onboard as my assistant—hugs and kisses to you!

As always, love to my family, especially my husband, Norm, for his unwavering faith in me, and to my "regulars": Lori, Donna, Shawn, and Norine.

Made in the USA
Middletown, DE
02 November 2023